THE RELIGION WAR

THE
RELIGION
WAR

SCOTT ADAMS

**Andrews McMeel
Publishing**

Kansas City

04 05 06 07 08 KP1 10 9 8 7 6 5 4 3 2 1

Library of Congress Cataloging-in-Publication Data

Adams, Scott, 1957–
   The religion war / Scott Adams.
      p. cm.
   Sequel to: God's debris.
    ISBN 0-7407-4788-6
     1. Christianity and other religions—Islam—Fiction. 2. Islam—Relations—Christianity—Fiction. 3. War—Religious aspects—Fiction. I. Title.

     PS3551.D395314R45 2004
     813'.54—dc22

2004047726

For one seven-pointer
from another

CONTENTS

CONTENTS

INTRODUCTION

This is a sequel to my book *God's Debris,* a story about a deliveryman who chances upon the smartest person in the world and learns the secrets of reality. I subtitled that book *A Thought Experiment* and used a variety of hypnosis techniques in an attempt to produce a feeling of euphoric enlightenment in the reader similar to what the main character would feel while discovering the (fictionally) true nature of reality. Reactions to the book were all over the map. About half of the people who e-mailed me said they felt various flavors of euphoria, expanded awareness, connectedness, and other weird sensations that defied description. A surprising number of people reported reading the entire book twice in one day. So I know *something* was happening. But no two people had the same reaction.

Other people wrote angry letters and scathing reviews, pointing out the logical and factual flaws in the book. It *is* full of flaws, and much of the science is made up, as it states in the introduction. I explained that the reader is *supposed to be looking for flaws.* That's what makes the experiment work. You might think this group of readers skipped the introduction and missed the stated point of the book, but I suspect that something else is going on. People get a kind of cognitive dissonance (brain cramp) when their worldview is disturbed. It's fun to watch.

The most interesting readers are the ones who have instant amnesia after reading the book, angrily insisting that there were *no new ideas* in it. False memories are a common side effect of having your worldview suddenly bent. You might love the book, you might hate it, but if you can *remember* it, you'll be interested to hear that some readers thought it had *no new ideas*.

The Religion War is a different kind of book. It's written in traditional fiction form with a plot (yes, a plot!) involving the smartest man in the world trying to stop a pending war between Christian and Muslim forces. The story takes you forward a few decades, to imagine where our current delusions about reality might lead us. And in the end it poses some questions that I think you'll enjoy rolling around in your head and jabbering about with friends while sipping a beverage. It's not essential that you first read *God's Debris,* but you will find this book more enjoyable if you do.

My target readers for *The Religion War* are bright people with short attention spans, especially lazy students and busy book clubs. I try to avoid tedious descriptions of scenery and clothing. I hope you don't miss them. You can read the whole thing in three hours, and it's packed with ideas to mull.

While the story is fiction, most booksellers will list the book under nonfiction because its purpose is to highlight the most important—yet most ignored—questions in the world. I list some of those questions in the back of the book, but they won't make complete sense until you've finished the story. I call them "Questions to Ponder."

I hope you enjoy the book. Feel free to write to me at scottadams@aol.com to give your reaction. I can't respond to every message, but I try to read all of them.

PROLOGUE

In the year 2007, a brilliant and charismatic leader named al-Zee began his rise to power in the Palestinian territories. He was the architect of the Twenty-Year Plan for eliminating Israel, the success of which started a domino effect in the Middle East, as one Arab dictatorship after another fell, and their territories rolled into the Great Caliphate. Al-Zee's subjects, heady from an unbroken string of victories, demanded the spread of Islam to the rest of the world. Al-Zee understood that this was neither practical nor desirable, but to satisfy the appetite of his people he began an unending war of minor terror against the Christian-dominated world. The attacks were calculated to be large enough to look like progress, yet small enough to avoid provoking all-out war. Publicly he blamed renegade groups for the attacks. The Christian-dominated countries knew al-Zee was behind the bombings, but they depended on him for their oil, and wanted to avoid a larger war that would cripple their economies, and in all likelihood increase the number of bombings.

Terror weapons improved dramatically during al-Zee's rule. Anyone with a few hundred dollars could buy a satellite-guided model airplane capable of flying a hundred miles to deliver explosives to a precise target. Terrorists no longer needed to commit suicide, so the pool of volunteers was unlimited. Al-Zee was careful to avoid killing anyone important or destroying anything irreplaceable. It was a difficult balancing act, trying to wage small-scale war without provoking total war. The strategy worked, until 2040, when General Horatio Cruz came to power in the Christian Alliance.

OLD MAN

"Sir, there's an old man in the lobby. He wants to talk to—" General Cruz, a reddish rhino of a man, stopped his lanky aide in midsentence. Cruz didn't like interruptions. He didn't like a lot of things: committees, fools, ambiguity, or unknowns. Cruz's faith in God, and his battlefield victories, imbued him with a sense of self-confidence and clarity that made him a natural leader. He knew that God was on his side, that his career was divinely inspired. He believed that when an idea came to him without a trail, it was God's way of talking. Those qualities, plus his tactical genius, propelled Cruz to Secretary of War, a position that had evolved to include de facto control over all the armies of NATO.

Cruz used his eyes the same way he used everything else: like weapons. Lieutenant Ben Waters suddenly found himself in the crosshairs. It wasn't the first time Waters had seen that look. That sort of look, from a man who killed people for a living, would reduce most people to stuttering. Waters viewed it as information, nothing more.

Cruz had hand-picked Waters from a thousand candidates, not because of his test scores or his combat record, both unremarkable. It certainly wasn't Waters' personality, charitably described as remote. There was something else: At the age of eight, Ben Waters used the family shotgun to kill both of his parents. It was a small town, and the neighbors agreed that Ben saved his younger brother from an unimaginable fate. No charges were filed. Since then, the area of Ben Waters' brain that makes a person feel alive was a catastrophe of molecules. He never suffered from shame, offense, fear, humiliation, or failure. But neither could he feel joy. Waters plugged the hole in his soul with military emotions—loyalty, duty, and mission.

Cruz picked Waters as his aide because power is the midwife of temptation, and the general's power was unequaled, at least in the non-Muslim territories. So too were his temptations. He had never crossed the line from duty to self-interest, at least not in any grotesque way, but the urge was a low-grade fever. Cruz ordered Waters to carry a sidearm at all times. Officially, it was to protect Cruz from assassination. Unofficially, it was Cruz's way of protecting the world from Cruz.

Waters understood the meaning behind Cruz's death stare: A general on the verge of war doesn't need surprise guests. It was obvious to both of them that the old man downstairs should be removed immediately. But today wasn't a day when the obvious counted for much. "Maybe if you talked to him for one minute. He's old and—"

"Tell security to drag his ass out of there."

"That's the thing," Waters explained. "The guards left. They just took off."

"What do you mean, 'left'?" Cruz said, as his square face reddened and his eyes turned space-black.

Most people would have backed off, but Waters didn't feel fear—not of Cruz, not of anyone or anything. All he had was a sense of what to do next, and in this case it meant an explanation. "The old man started talking to the guards and five minutes later they left. They didn't say why."

"Call the Marines off the roof. If the old fool won't leave, shoot him."

"Yes, sir," said Waters, in a way that revealed he knew it wasn't a workable plan.

Waters walked deliberately out of the room, dragging his past like a bag of graveyard dirt, leaving Cruz to continue arranging his war map on a huge oval table.

"The whole world are fools," muttered Cruz while using a ruler to drag a battle platform from the Indian Ocean.

Mapmakers were a frustrated group. The old notion of a "country" was meaningless. Al-Zee dominated the entire Islamic world. Governments existed under his rule, in a fashion, to keep the water running, to remove garbage, and to run indoctrination centers for children, but the real power was al-Zee. In the Christian-dominated part of the world, there was still a pretense that civilian governments ruled their respective countries. In reality, Cruz had the power to redraw boundaries and remove so-called leaders with a word. He didn't need military power to get his way, although it was available if it suited him. Cruz was widely believed to be the only person who could stop the terror of al-Zee. No one felt it was a good idea to distract him.

The atheists and the smaller religions were lying low, supporting the Christian power base and enjoying safety in numbers. The most enthusiastic supporters of the Christians were the Jews who escaped Israel after al-Zee's forces overran it in 2035.

Battle platforms were a recent addition to Cruz's arsenal. They were the size of cities, floating on the ocean, vastly more powerful than the aircraft carriers they replaced. The platforms could be assembled in days, ringed by destroyers, and monitored by an umbrella of satellites. Nothing could penetrate their perimeters, thanks to NATO's technical breakthrough of forced particle beams that could slice through incoming metal like a hot poker on a cobweb. The rest of the world, which was mostly al-Zee's territories and a sprinkling of nonaligned powers, used conventional missiles that were no match for the particle beam defense grid.

Cruz moved one of his four battle platforms from the Indian Ocean to the Eastern Seaboard of the United States. It meant one less asset near the main battlefield, but it might make the civilian politicians more agreeable to his plans, knowing they'd be protected from incoming warheads. And once they got used to that protection, Cruz would have something to take away from them in case they forgot who was in charge.

This was a different sort of war from anything Cruz had fought before. He couldn't hope to cut off the snake's head to kill the body, as the media were fond of saying. The genius behind al-Zee's success was that he had weaponized a population of two billion people, most of them under the age of thirty, convincing them that death was better than life, so long as they died in service to al-Zee's interpretation of the afterlife.

There was a word that Cruz avoided using, but it was always in his mind. This wouldn't be a war for *territory* or *power*. It would be a war of *extermination*. Two billion souls would probably perish before it was over. Cruz prayed that the two billion were on the other side. He knew that if he gave himself up to God, God would guide him to victory.

The tall wooden doors of Cruz's war room opened to a stream of military advisers: admirals and generals. There were twenty-five of them, one from each of the dominant NATO countries. They had no decision-making power—Cruz had the monopoly on that. But they were useful in maintaining the illusion that NATO enjoyed some sort of democratic input. It was thin fiction, the sort that a wartime population was happy to accept. The Joint Chiefs of Staff for the United States had become overdressed advisers, symbolic and useless. The NATO generals were more loyal to Cruz than to their own civilian governments. In times of extreme danger, an extreme man like Cruz didn't need to grab power; it surrendered to him.

The admirals and generals were a concert of leather and pressed cotton; their medals and shoes played percussion as they took their positions around the black oval map table. Admiral Helms, a tall drawn skeleton of a man, had an uncharacteristically troubled expression. The others looked at him, waiting for him to say something.

"There's an old man in the lobby," Admiral Helms said, looking at Cruz. "He wants to talk to you."

Cruz paused a moment, trying to rein in his anger. He took a long breath and scanned the now-worried faces of the group. When he locked on to Helms' face, he exploded. "Why the hell do you think I care about some fool in the lobby? Have you lost your mind?!"

Cruz went on in that vein for a full minute, spitting out every irritation and frustration of the past week, and focusing it all on the withering Admiral Helms. Cruz was on a roll, his words like napalm, until the tall wooden doors opened again. It was the captain of the Marine guard. "Excuse me, sir. I'm sorry to interrupt."

Cruz turned on the captain, brandishing his most intense "this better be good" look.

"There's an old man in the lobby. He says he wants to see you."

Cruz looked at the captain for a beat and then cranked around to face Helms. "Someone better tell me what's so special about this fool in the lobby. And it better happen right now."

Helms tried. "I thought he was a street person when I first saw him outside the building. He doesn't have a jacket, just a red plaid blanket that looks pretty beat up. But there's something about him. I said hi, and the next thing I knew he was describing our entire battle plan as if he'd been in every meeting with us."

"So what!" Cruz yelled. "The media have been spraying it all over the news for the past six months. Every moron knows our plans!"

"No, I mean he knows the *specifics*. He described our exact troop deployment plans, our attack sequence, exactly where we're planning to stage our battle platforms."

"Except for one of the platforms," piped in General Franken.

"Yes," Helms agreed. "He said that one of the battle platforms would be off Washington, D.C. He got that wrong, but he knew so much about the rest, and that struck me as—"

Helms' sentence was cut short by the crash of the oval map table, overturned by a raging General Cruz. "Stop him in the lobby!" Cruz barked at the Marine captain, then followed him toward the elevator. Cruz passed Lieutenant Waters in the outer office and grabbed him by the arm of his shirt, dragging him the first few yards.

In the elevator, Cruz snatched the captain's M-16 and flipped off the safety. The captain drew his sidearm. Waters watched, not knowing where they were going or why. He wasn't worried. He didn't know how to worry.

"Little bastard. He's up to something," Cruz muttered, watching the floor indicators illuminate in reverse order as they neared the lobby. "He'd better hope he's one of ours. Otherwise he's going to have a long day."

Cruz was the first one through the elevator door, dispersing a surprised group of government employees. Janet Redmond tripped on her own shoes trying to back out of the way. An intelligence analyst caught her before she hit the ground. A half-scream was all she could muster before fear muffled it. The most powerful wartime general in history was hurried and mad. Nothing good could come from that. Cruz never looked in Janet Redmond's direction. He bulled his way into the lobby, with the M-16 pointed toward the ceiling, scanning for the man in the blanket.

"He's gone," the captain said.

"Get my car. I'm evacuating immediately. Keep the NATO chiefs in the war room. Don't sound a general alarm. I'll be in the garage in two minutes."

"Sir?" the captain asked.

Cruz filled in the blanks while continuing to survey the lobby in all directions. "Someone on my staff—someone in that room—is leaking war plans. We're going to put some distance between that old man and me, because this smells wrong. Once command and control is secured, I'll deal with the leak and the old man. Get the car."

The captain left in a sprint. Waters, having pieced together only part of the story, said, "I'll get the portable."

The portable was their name for a handheld command and control device that followed Cruz wherever he went. It was unjammable, nearly indestructible. When the user entered an access code and a GPS location, and specified a payload, a missile would arrive on that spot soon after, launched from a site in South Dakota that fewer than a dozen people on Earth knew about.

Waters and Cruz bundled into the open door of the bullet-proof limousine. The driver stomped the gas pedal, forcing the concrete floor into a scream as the limo's door closed from the acceleration. The newly arrived occupants felt themselves pressed against the backseat.

The driver, Rick Ames, had trained eighteen years for this moment. He was an expert at escape and evasion. Until now, it had always been on the practice courses. Adrenaline surged into his bloodstream until he could hear his own heartbeat. The huge steel bomb door at the top of the ramp opened as the tanklike limo accelerated toward the gaping hole. At the top of the ramp stood a man, his features obliterated by the shock of daylight that enveloped him and poured into the garage, down the ramp, and into three pairs of eyes. Ames slowed the car for half a beat, trying to get a read on the situation, to size up the threat, to reprogram his exit strategy if needed.

"Hit him!" Cruz ordered.

That was all the information Ames needed; he punched the gas pedal and closed the distance between four tons of solid mass and the smallish figure ahead. In the next few seconds, the minds of Cruz and Waters and Ames were flooded with images of light and color and sound, mixed with their own brain chemistries. None of them perceived the same thing. Cruz saw the man lean his head back and raise his arms over his head; then as the car reached striking distance, the man fell backwards, disappearing under the view of the hood—crushed, he figured. There was a distinct thud sound, but Cruz wondered if it was just the tires bouncing back to the pavement after being launched at the top of the ramp.

Waters noticed that the old man was wearing some sort of deliveryman's shirt, threadbare, with a name tag on the breast. Behind him was a red plaid blanket spread on the ground as if to host a picnic. He was the man from the lobby. Waters' flashback of the earlier conversation in the lobby merged with the image he saw in front of him until memory and perception lost their boundaries.

Ames fixated on the man's eyes, seeing almost nothing else. They were ancient eyes. He felt as if he could drive his car directly into those orbs and emerge at some other part of the universe. Ames didn't feel pity, and he wondered why. Was it the training or the certainty of what he had to do? Or was there something in those eyes that forgave him in advance? The eyes had no fear, no hate, and no surprise. Suddenly the eyelids closed, blocking Ames' escape route. He felt a surge of panic as though he were the first person to find out about the end of the world. He screamed and squeezed the steering wheel to steady against the impact and the horror that would follow. But he felt nothing. Nor should he have, because four tons of soundproofed steel will make short work of 150 pounds of man. He didn't look in his mirror for confirmation, preferring not to have that image in his mind for the rest of his life.

The tank–limo took a hard right turn outside the building, bowling Cruz, Waters, and the portable into the left side door. Ames accelerated toward H2, the emergency headquarters.

Cruz pressed a button that slid a barrier in place between the driver and passengers. Then he grabbed the portable from the floor of the limo and punched in the unlock code, revealing an elaborate control panel with a display screen. Cruz glanced at Waters, looking for a reaction, and saw nothing save his usual indecipherable blankness. Cruz punched in the GPS coordinates of the Department of Defense building they had just left, where the NATO representatives were still waiting, clueless about what had transpired in the past three minutes. Cruz selected a payload large enough to level the building, but not much more, and looked again at Waters. The lieutenant had shifted his position to free up his service revolver, or maybe it was just to be more comfortable, or maybe to better see. Cruz couldn't tell. He let Waters see exactly what he was doing on the portable.

"Why?" Waters asked.

It wasn't much of a reaction, but it was something. Cruz preferred feeling resistance no matter what he was doing, so he could enjoy the feeling of plowing it aside. "Someone back there is a mole. That's the only way the old man could have known our exact battle plans. I don't have time to find out who it is, and frankly, it doesn't matter. I don't need any of them. Hell, the world is better off if I don't have to stop and explain every bullet to those idiots."

"How do you plan to explain it to the world?" Waters asked calmly, as if requesting an extra slice of cheese on a sandwich.

"I won't have to explain anything. The world will assume it was an attack from one of al-Zee's fanatics."

Cruz was right. Hundreds of buildings had blown up in the past two years alone. The military had stopped analyzing the remains of each explosion long ago, assuming correctly that they all were the work of al-Zee. No one would request an inquiry about this blast because al-Zee would be the universally presumed perpetrator.

Cruz knew that this explosion would extinguish the last shred of pacifism from the Christian world. He would have complete freedom to prosecute the war as he pleased. No committees. No second-guessing. Just certainty. He needed that now because his plans for extermination would not survive a consensus vote.

"They're soldiers," Cruz said, trying to justify himself. "This is what they signed up for. They don't get to choose who kills them or why."

Cruz thrived in this sort of situation. It was what set him apart from other leaders. Minutes earlier he had identified a grave threat. Now he was one button away from turning the situation to his advantage. He viewed all destruction as opportunity.

Waters let his right hand drop down to the seat next to his service weapon. Cruz got the message, and responded with more explanation. This was a line that Cruz had never crossed. He had killed his share of people who, in his opinion, deserved killing. He had sent his own troops on missions from which he knew they wouldn't return. But this was different. "This is global war, Lieutenant. There are no rules, except the ones you invent and live to talk about. If we're not willing to kill our own soldiers to gain an advantage in this war, we're no match for al-Zee."

"None of the generals were in the room when you moved the battle platform near Washington," Waters pointed out, having noticed the change himself when he first entered the room to announce the old man in the lobby.

Cruz stared at him, furious that he hadn't realized it himself. Waters had a point. No one could have told the old man about the latest change. Maybe the old man made a lucky guess. Clearly it wasn't *all* luck, because the old man was said to know the battle plans in detail.

"Waters, tell me the world will be better if the NATO generals live. Then I won't push the button. Tell me you think that running a war with twenty-five hens pecking at my ankles, second-guessing every decision, getting their locals all stirred up—tell me that's the best way to win this war."

Waters' expression masked whatever was happening in his mind. He just listened, not rejecting, not agreeing.

"How many times have I sent men into situations where I knew they wouldn't come back? That's the soldier's lot. If his death makes the war easier to win, he dies. This is no different. Al-Zee doesn't make his decisions by committee. The only way we're going to kick his ass back into the cave is if I run this war the way it's meant to be run. That means one leader, no second-guessing."

Cruz paused to see the impact of his argument.

"Tell me I'm wrong, damn it! That's an order!" he barked.

"How do you know *I'm* not the mole? I know your battle plans too," Waters said.

Cruz stared into Waters' empty eyes, looking for a sign of fear or anger or anything that would be a clue. As usual, there was nothing. "I *don't* know for sure that you're not the mole," said Cruz, not liking where this line of thought led.

"Whether or not I'm the mole, you have a bigger problem. If you kill the NATO leaders, I'll know you did it. You'll always have that hanging over you; I'll have the power to bring you down. You'll have to kill me too just to know the secret is safe."

Waters made sense. Cruz didn't have an immediate answer, but none was needed because he felt Waters' sidearm pressed to his temple.

"Give me the portable," Waters said calmly.

Cruz moved his eyes but not his head. This was trouble. Cruz reasoned that his best chance of getting out of this situation was to comply, for now, and hope his instinct provided him with a next step. Waters slid the portable off Cruz's lap and onto his own, gun still pressed firmly on the general's temple. Waters looked down at the portable and clicked the Confirm button, engaging the missile. Within seconds a silo in South Dakota glided open and spit out its angry cargo toward a building full of NATO generals and admirals.

Waters holstered his sidearm, closed the portable, and put it back in its case. Cruz just watched, not sure what had happened, his silence begging the question.

"Now I don't have anything on you," Waters said. "And if I were the mole, you'd already be dead."

Cruz was enraged, but he still appreciated the ingenuity of Waters' solution. "Remind me to promote you. And then remind me to put a boot up your ass."

EMERGENCY
HEADQUARTERS

As Cruz's limo pulled into H2, the airwaves were crackling with stories about the destruction of the Defense Department building. The steel blast gate closed behind them as a dozen soldiers surrounded the limo and leveled their weapons at the occupants. They knew it was Cruz's limo, but they were taught to suspect the worst. Nothing came into or out of H2 without challenge. There was no way to know who was with the general, or what their intentions were. Cruz, Waters, and Ames put their hands behind their heads as the guards opened the doors, pulled them out, and inserted the bomb-sniffing sensors.

Waters and Ames were patted down and disarmed immediately. A soldier approached Cruz to do the same but thought better of it, saluting and moving aside. Waters, his identity confirmed, was rearmed and followed Cruz toward the main control room. Cruz's presence scattered people in the hallway, pressing them against the walls, like a destroyer class ship moving through a koi pond. Everyone had heard the news and they knew the implications: Cruz was one war away from controlling most of the world.

Cruz exploded into the control room and barked to the staff, each of them stiffened by his entrance, "Get me on the bird!"

Technicians worked ferociously to eliminate the risk of being asked, "What's taking so long?" They knew the drill. Within minutes Cruz's voice and face would be broadcast onto every television and radio station in the Christian-allied world. The system had been used only a few times, always for emergencies. This qualified.

Cruz placed himself on a black leather chair in front of a remote-controlled camera. A technician floated in and attached a microphone to his shirt. A disembodied voice counted down from ten, the room fell silent, lights dimmed except on Cruz, and the camera's red light glowed.

Cruz spoke. "I am General Horatio Cruz, High Commander of NATO. Minutes ago the Defense Department building, along with the military heads of twenty-five NATO countries, was the target of a cowardly attack by—most people believe—al-Zee. I have survived and will see to it that the defense of our countries is not compromised by the temporary gap in command structure. In a few days I will announce my plans for ending this struggle with the forces of al-Zee. I know I can count on the support of each of your nations. That is all for now."

Cruz unhooked his microphone and stood up before the red camera light went out, in a calculated move to show the world he was a man of action, a man who knew exactly what to do. And he felt that way, too. He had a clearly defined enemy, a battle plan, and now no second-guessers. His head was unusually clear. God was obviously on his side, guiding him. Cruz liked that feeling. It lasted exactly four seconds.

A captain cautiously approached Cruz and said, "There's an old man in the lobby, with a blanket. He says he wants to talk to you."

Cruz's forehead turned purple with rage. But he wasn't going to lose it now, not here, not in front of his men. He knew that everything he said or did for the next few days would be the subject of history books for centuries. Worse, if he got a reputation for being irrational, it would make it harder for him to order people into harm's way. Now was the time for cool, no matter how much effort that required. Cruz took a deep breath before speaking.

"Take him to I-Wing. Find out who he's working for and how he knows what he knows. Don't kill him until you're sure he's telling the truth."

I-Wing was the interrogation center at H2. During wartime, or anything that looked like wartime, all rules of interrogation were suspended. No one who entered I-Wing ever left, so the Christian-allied world remained blissfully ignorant of the work being done on its behalf. They enjoyed the pleasant fiction that only the other side perpetrated atrocities. The bad guys *tortured*. The good guys only *interrogated*. Except that no one ever saw a picture of anyone who had recently been *interrogated*.

INTERROGATION

The Avatar was sixty-two years old but could have been mistaken for ninety, gaunt, clad in a threadbare deliveryman's outfit from an earlier time. His silver-gray hair was short and untamed. A red plaid blanket covered his shoulders, clutched tight in front.

Thirty years ago, as a package deliveryman, he met the prior Avatar, from whom he learned the secrets that brought him to the fifth level of awareness, but it took a terrible toll on his body. Humans are not genetically equipped to handle this kind of knowledge, and he was no exception. The awareness aged him prematurely. He understood too much about reality, and with that knowledge came an overwhelming responsibility, and an incalculable stress that spread to every cell of his body.

He was rich beyond imagination and lived a hermit life in a Victorian home in San Francisco. Most of his money was inherited from the prior Avatar, according to the Avatar tradition. The rest of his fortune was made by investing, using his unparalleled ability to recognize patterns before they fully developed.

He was painfully lonely. The last Avatar hadn't advised him to avoid personal relationships; it was just obvious that he had to. No one could understand the pressures he endured. He could no longer talk to normal people without leaving them changed in some way. It was unfair, he thought, to change a person for no reason. No ordinary person could understand what it was like to be an Avatar, so even when he did talk to people, when it was absolutely necessary, he was still utterly alone.

He felt as though he was one short gasp from insanity. Most of the time he felt certain that he had a special role to play, that he was *chosen,* that he alone could save the world from the upcoming destruction. Other times he felt he must surely be mad, because only insane people think like that. And they, as did he, have no capacity to know which category they really belong to.

On this topic, as on so many others, there was no one he could talk to. The Avatar knew he needed to keep to himself, to suffer in silence. In the end, he expected that the loneliness would kill him before the knowledge ate him from the inside. Solitude was his personal monster.

The pressure was sometimes so great that he fantasized about trying to tell someone exactly who and what he was, hoping to ease the pain of isolation. But when he imagined the conversation, he would visualize the face of the other person losing its smile and taking on an expression of fear, or pity, or loathing. There is no way to explain to someone that you are the keeper of reality, the one most aware, the guardian of God's intent. So he kept it to himself, and he let it age him.

He knew that someday he would find his replacement, but only when his body failed. It wasn't time for that. He had work to do. This was why he existed, or perhaps it was the surest sign of his insanity. In honest moments of reflection, he didn't know which.

"I'm sorry. Really, I am," said the Avatar, cuffed to the wall in I-Wing.

"For what—getting caught?" growled the thick-necked interrogator with an oversize forehead and stubby fingers, as he moved his cart full of pain-tools nearer his subject.

"I'm sorry for what I have to do."

"This will end quickly if you tell me everything," said the interrogator.

"That's why I'm here: to tell you everything."

"Then we're going to get along great," said the interrogator, as he plugged an electronic device into a wall outlet, tapping two electrodes together to spark them unnecessarily, making a point.

"I won't enjoy this," said the Avatar.

"That's the understatement of the century," said the interrogator.

"There's never enough time to do things right," said the Avatar. "I don't blame you personally. You just happen to be in the wrong place at the wrong time. I'm in a hurry and I don't have the luxury of doing things in a more civilized way."

"Acting crazy don't work in here, blanket-man. I've seen all the tricks. Playing the loon is chapter one in the stop-hurting-me book. It ain't even clever. In fact, truth be told, I'm insulted that you'd even try."

"I'm sure you're very good at your work. I didn't mean to imply otherwise," said the Avatar. "May we start soon?"

"What's that—reverse psychology? Again, you insult me."

The Avatar sighed and muttered another apology that was lost.

"Before I turn your guts into jam, how about you tell me everything I need to know. It's a little courtesy I like to extend to my guests. No one has ever taken me up on the offer, but I feel it's only fair to put it out there. Let's say that you figure out what questions I need to ask and then you just answer them. If you make me ask the obvious questions over and over, I'm going to get tired. And that makes me cranky. You don't want that."

"Very well," replied the Avatar. "And again, I am truly sorry."

"Talk or get scrambled. It's your choice, old man," said the interrogator.

"Hypothetically," said the Avatar, "if you met someone who literally knew everything, would that person appear sane to you?"

"Are you saying you know everything?" asked the interrogator. "If you do, we're going to be here a long time."

"I'm just asking, if such a person existed, someone who knew the answers to the important questions of life, such as why we're here, what's our purpose, then how could you recognize that person as the real thing?"

"If he was so smart, then everything he said would make sense. It wouldn't be too hard to know he was the real deal."

"You would think so, but look around you. The armies of al-Zee believe that the founder of their religion rode to paradise on a flying horse. Their enemies, the Christians, believe that no horses have ever flown. They can't both be right. At best, only one version is true. Either a horse flew or it didn't. People can't seem to agree on something as simple as flying horses, so how good are people at recognizing deeper truths when they see them?"

"Okay, I get it. Now you'll tell me that you're the smartest person in the universe so I shouldn't hurt you. Well, I gotta give you credit for originality. That's one I haven't heard."

The Avatar studied the interrogator, noticing a chain around his neck, the sort that often holds a cross. His features and coloring suggested a genetic path through Ireland. His teeth were crooked on the bottom, and he had remnants of acne scars from his youth, revealing a childhood of modest means. His movements were graceless, bordering on awkward. He had the first sign of drinker's nose. His eyes were tired and pillowed. His posture was a tale of dark happenings over a lifetime.

"Tell me something brilliant, old man," mocked the interrogator. "Convince me that you're the smartest man in the world and I'll let you go."

"I don't think the smartest man in the world would believe that you're sincere."

The interrogator flashed an executioner's grin and turned up the voltage. He moved the electric paddles toward the old man's chest.

"This is just to get your attention. Do me a favor and don't die right away."

"Who is Patrick?" asked the Avatar.

The interrogator froze for a moment, then quick-boiled. "How do you know my brother? What kind of bullshit is this? What else do you know about me?"

The old man looked into the eyes of his interrogator and took a deep breath. "I know that you were raised Catholic, but as an adult you pick and choose the parts you want to believe. You think it's okay to hurt people as long as it's in the interest of the greater good. You convinced yourself that you'd still go to heaven, so long as you accept Jesus before you die. You were treated unkindly as a child, especially by the older boys and by the better athletes. You don't sleep much, because every time you close your eyes you see your victims. You hear their voices, just before you drift off to sleep, and it pulls you back to restlessness. Sometimes you try to stop the voices by drinking. The drinking works, to a point, but it has ruined your relationships."

The interrogator dropped the paddles and stepped away from the old man.

"What's your name?" asked the interrogator.

"Avatar."

"Do I know you?"

"Not as well as I know you," said the Avatar.

"How do you know so much about me?" asked the interrogator.

"It's called a 'cold read,'" answered the Avatar.

"You're freaking me out. It's time for you to stop jacking me around," said the interrogator, picking up the paddles.

For centuries, phony psychics have used a version of the *cold read* to dupe gullible customers. It is nothing but good observations combined with educated guesses and generalities, but it seems like so much more to the person hearing it. Some fake psychics were unusually skilled at noticing clues from a person's appearance or mannerisms and making guesses that sounded uncannily accurate. The Avatar was the best of the best, able to recognize patterns so subtle that even the most skilled phony psychic would have found it amazing. Today's situation was especially easy. The interrogator was clearly Irish. Someone in his family was probably named Patrick. He was probably Catholic, judging from the chain around his neck. He probably experienced guilt about his job. He probably drank, judging from his appearance and his occupation.

"May I continue?" asked the Avatar.

The interrogator nodded uneasily, and the Avatar continued. "Sometimes, especially when you've been drinking, you wonder if there's any point in living. You think about ending your life. You aren't sure what's stopping you."

The interrogator placed the electrodes on the cart and clicked the Off button. He crossed his arms, his posture revealing that he was both angry and interested.

The Avatar continued, "You think about the risk of going to hell if you kill yourself, versus the odds that hell is just a fairy tale to scare people into good behavior. You wonder if God would forgive a suicide. You figure the stakes are too high to take a chance. You wish you had someone to talk with about your urge, but you think people would see you as damaged goods if you let your feelings out. It would affect your career and still not give you the certainty you crave."

"You're a bastard," said the interrogator.

"I hear that a lot," said the Avatar. "One more thing: Your arm itches," said the Avatar, merging his knowledge of hypnosis with the cold read to make it more powerful. The interrogator was now in a highly suggestible frame of mind, boggled by the seeming accuracy of the Avatar's insights, though they were little more than observation and pattern recognition. The human brain doesn't like confusion. It will seek the relief of certainty wherever it can find it, even if it has to hallucinate to do so. The Avatar was keeping the interrogator in a mentally uncomfortable position, preparing him to crave the certainty that the Avatar would provide.

The interrogator stared at the Avatar, trying not to blink, trying harder to ignore the itch forming on his right arm. The seconds passed painfully until the silence was broken by the sound of scratching and cursing. The door to the interrogator's subconscious swung open.

"You're a collection of molecules," the Avatar explained, his manner now serious, "and those molecules are made of smaller bits, and those bits are made of even smaller bits. The smallest bits in the universe are all identical. You are made of the same stuff as the concrete in the floor and the fly on the window. Your basic matter cannot be created or destroyed. All that will survive of what you call your life is the sum of your actions. Some might call the unending ripple effect of those actions a soul, or a spirit."

"What's your point?" asked the interrogator, more confused than ever.

"Had I not met you today, you would continue to hurt people until your body lost its coherence and your dust was loaned back to the universe. Every day that you're alive causes harm to the universe, and you are aware of it. It eats you because your most basic nature is to contribute to your species, not work against it. Your life is a losing battle against a million years of evolution."

The interrogator listened, and paced. He said nothing, wishing for mental comfort but finding none in the Avatar's point about tiny bits of matter and evolution. It occurred to him that he needed the answer to a bigger question, perhaps THE BIGGEST QUESTION. Maybe this Avatar fellow knew the answer; he seemed to know so much about other things—things that a person couldn't know. The interrogator paused, took a breath, then looked directly at the Avatar. "Is there a God?"

The Avatar smiled. "In a manner of speaking."

"How can you be so sure? Half the guys in my unit are atheists. They don't seem so dumb. Maybe they're right."

"After you have released my arms, I will be happy to explain it to you," offered the Avatar, using another common hypnosis technique, making the interrogator focus on what happens *after* the arms are released, leapfrogging the question of *whether* they *should* be.

The interrogator weighed the odds that this old man could escape the room, shackled or not. The door was locked from the outside, and the interrogator had a sidearm. His curiosity was piqued. He had searched his whole life for a better argument about the existence of God—either for or against—and he had a feeling this old man could move that argument. If not, he could always kill him later. Suddenly there seemed to be no hurry.

The unrestrained Avatar sat on a stool and stretched his arms. The interrogator pulled up a metal chair, keeping a safe distance. "Okay, tell me how you're so sure that God exists."

"Sometimes what seems to be a difference in opinions is in fact just a difference in definitions," explained the Avatar. "Defined carefully, atheists and believers all accept the existence of the same God."

"What kind of crap is that?" growled the interrogator. "Atheists don't believe in any kind of God. That's the whole point of being an atheist. Start making sense."

"My claim," said the Avatar, "is that I can define God in a way that both believers and nonbelievers will agree upon, proving in the process that their differences are only a matter of trivial details."

"My claim is that you're full of baloney," said the interrogator.

"If I can prove my point to your satisfaction, will you release me?" asked the Avatar.

"No. If I don't do my job with you, they don't let *me* out. The last thing Cruz needs is an interrogator leaving the reservation. If the guard outside that door gets a whiff that I'm turning soft, he's got orders to wax me."

"I'm sorry," said the Avatar. "I really am."

"Get back to the point, old man. Define God so an atheist believes in it. I gotta hear this."

"The secret is time," said the Avatar. "My definition of God is acceptable to everyone if they can allow some flexibility in the scope of time. And I think you'd agree that an omnipotent being would not be operating on a predetermined schedule. If it took God one day or a trillion years to accomplish something, it would make no difference to him."

"Okay, God doesn't have a watch. I get that," said the interrogator.

"Tell me what qualities you believe God has," directed the Avatar.

"Well . . . obviously he's all-powerful. And he's everywhere. And he loves people, or so they say, although I haven't seen much evidence of that."

"Is he conscious?" asked the Avatar.

"Yeah, he's gotta be conscious. I don't want you getting away with saying that God is physics or natural laws or some crap like that. He's gotta be able to think and to have plans."

"Very well," said the Avatar. "I will define God in a way that meets all of your tests."

"I'm listening," said the interrogator, leaning back in his chair, legs crossed at the knees.

"God is all the matter in the universe, and all the blank spaces, and the probability that anything exists in any place at any time. That is the full definition," said the Avatar.

"You'd better have more than that, old man. How's that explain any of the powers of God?"

"It explains *all* of God's powers, simply and completely. God hides in plain sight," explained the Avatar.

"That explains nothing," argued the interrogator. "That's just a bunch of mumbo jumbo."

"What powers of God does it overlook?"

"Well, for one, God's gotta be everywhere at the same time, and your definition is . . . well . . ." The interrogator's voice trailed off. "Okay, I see. If God is all the stuff in the universe, then he's everywhere. But that's the *only* power that fits your definition. I mean, what about being all-knowing?"

"Do you know how information is stored on a computer?" asked the Avatar.

"Sure. It's a bunch of zeros and ones," answered the interrogator. "You just have to put them in the right order."

"Likewise, the universe has two fundamental conditions: There is only matter and empty space. Every part of the universe is a sequence of matter and empty space. All meaningful patterns of zeros and ones are stored in the universe, making it, in effect, all-knowing."

"That's crap," protested the interrogator. "First of all, you can't be sure that every pattern of ones and zeros exists in the universe.

Secondly, you can't compare a bunch of random particles in an asteroid with information that's created by intelligent beings. And third, even if a pattern *is* in the universe, say in a teacup handle, it's not retrievable, so it's not the same thing as real knowledge."

The Avatar was pleased with the level of interest the interrogator showed. "Would you agree that if you could make the universe any size you wanted, with no constraints whatsoever—say a trillion times larger than you imagine it to be—that eventually you would get a pattern in some corner of the universe that was the equal, in ones and zeros, to all of Shakespeare's plays?"

"No, I don't agree. Maybe the simple patterns are out there, but not the more complicated ones. It's just too unlikely."

"Complicated patterns are nothing but simple patterns combined. For example, if you know that a monkey can be trained, and you understand the concept of a hat, you already know you can probably train a monkey to wear a hat, even if that information does not yet exist anywhere in the universe. Knowledge is the potential to bring simple information into consciousness and combine it," explained the Avatar.

"It has to be more than potential," said the interrogator.

"Does it? Consider your own so-called knowledge. Your conscious mind uses only the tiniest scoop of your total knowledge—whatever you are thinking at the moment. Everything else that you *know* is just an arrangement of matter in your brain that could *potentially* be retrieved but most of it never will. For example, your brain might contain the name of a grade school acquaintance that you will never again think about. You would consider that *knowledge* even though it will never be retrieved. Your own knowledge is similar to the universe's knowledge, mostly *potential,* not actual."

"You're making my head hurt. I'm not sure I'm following all this, but I know you have a huge hole in your thinking. There's no consciousness controlling all of this random stuff in the universe. You can't have God without consciousness," said the interrogator.

"Define 'consciousness,' " responded the Avatar.

"Well, you know, it's when you're conscious. You know what you're doing and you feel you're doing stuff intentionally," tried the interrogator.

"So you have a sensation of consciousness. Fair enough. But how do you know if *I'm* conscious? Can you tell by observing me?" asked the Avatar.

"Not really. I just assume you're a human like me, so you must have consciousness too."

"So how would you know God was conscious, even if he stood in front of you?" asked the Avatar.

"Hmmm." The interrogator paused, gathering his thoughts. "I guess I couldn't tell from his actions, because there's no way to know how God would react to any situation. I mean, he wouldn't be afraid or hungry or curious, so he'd have no obvious motives to compare against what he did. I guess the only way I'd know is if he decided to tell me he was conscious, probably through some kind of messenger or angel or prophet or something."

"Allow me to give you a more workable definition of consciousness," said the Avatar.

"Okay," said the interrogator, sitting back in his chair, relieved.

"You say you know you're conscious because you have the sensation of consciousness, although you can't quite put your finger on it. Let's agree that the sensation is part of the package, but only a by-product," said the Avatar.

"What else is there?" asked the interrogator.

"Consciousness is a feedback loop," explained the Avatar. "It has four parts: You imagine the impact of your action, then you act, then you observe the actual result of your action, then you store that knowledge in your brain and begin again to imagine the next thing. All of those steps have a physical component, including the imagining—meaning that your brain is having chemical and electrical activity—so it's no wonder that you have a sensation that you call consciousness," explained the Avatar.

"You make it sound so simple," said the interrogator.

"Does it sound wrong?" asked the Avatar.

"No. I just hadn't thought about it before," confessed the interrogator.

"So then, if the universe exhibited the four steps that define consciousness in humans, would it be fair to say the universe as a whole is conscious?" asked the Avatar.

The interrogator paused for a moment before nodding a reluctant agreement.

"And would you agree that it's sufficient for this God consciousness to be located someplace in the universe—just as your consciousness is located in your brain and not in your elbow?" asked the Avatar.

"Okay," agreed the interrogator.

"Consider the collective actions of all the humans in the world," said the Avatar. "Would you agree that we imagine things—as a group—before acting?"

"No. Humans imagine things as individuals," said the interrogator, trying to hold his ground.

"You imagine *some* things as individuals, such as what you plan to have for lunch. But you have shared imagination for the bigger things, such as imagining what it would be like to cure cancer. Society's imagination is collective, with the more informed individual imaginations feeding into the whole, broadcast by the media, and changing the collective imagination by changing all of the individuals that compose it."

"Okay," agreed the interrogator. "So you're saying that God's consciousness is the sum of human consciousness. But how do you explain love? God loves us, right? Where's the love in your random universe?"

"Will you accept that God's form of love is a *better* version than human love?"

"I don't know about that. I've never felt either kind, so I'm no judge."

"Would God feel jealous, or needy, or vulnerable with his version of love?" asked the Avatar.

"No, I guess not," conceded the interrogator.

"So for God, it's a streamlined phenomenon, this love. It has none of the ugly baggage of human love."

"I guess so."

"For God, love is the highest level of preference. That which God prefers the most, he also loves the most. If you consider all of the patterns of matter and space that could exist, it is amazingly unlikely that human beings would emerge. And so it could be said that the probabilities governing the universe have displayed a preference for life over nonliving matter. Over time, the amount of life is increasing, while the total nonliving portions of the universe shrink as a percentage."

"So you're saying that God must love people because he's making more of them and not making more dirt?"

"Essentially, yes. When you remove the pain and baggage of love, you are left with *preference* as the only accurate indicator of love."

"That kinda makes sense, because people want to spend the most time with the people they love the most," agreed the interrogator.

"Have I made my case?" asked the Avatar.

The interrogator looked away, pausing overlong before responding. "I'm sorry I have to kill you, old man. I don't know if you're the smartest person in the world or not, but I will admit I'm not ruling it out. This is gonna be the hardest thing I've ever done."

"If it's any comfort, you won't be killing me," said the Avatar.

"How's that?" asked the interrogator, the energy drained from his voice.

"I'm afraid I've fiddled with your subconscious, unblocking it. You'll be doing God's work today," said the Avatar.

"I doubt that."

"Consider what's going on outside this building. Calculate the cost of a battle between al-Zee and Cruz. How many will die?" asked the Avatar.

"A billion. Maybe more," said the interrogator, sinking deeper into his chair.

"Unless something stops it."

"Nothing can stop it," said the interrogator. "It's happening."

"If you had the chance, would you give your life to stop it?" asked the Avatar.

"I wish I had that power."

"I came here to meet General Cruz, to stop the war," explained the Avatar. "You will share in that journey when you set me free. It is the point and purpose of your life."

As the Avatar planned, the interrogator's conscious mind was scrambled by the emotions and thoughts of the past minutes. This brutish man, accustomed to avoiding deep thoughts, had imagined the tiniest particles of the universe, his childhood, and the battles of the future. He had laughed, felt pain and pity, been intellectually stimulated, confused, assured, and uncertain. The Avatar had challenged his worldview, and it was evaporating, leaving him feeling empty, unimportant, and purposeless.

He needed to stop the pain. Maybe if he killed the Avatar quickly, that would help. The interrogator stared openmouthed at the Avatar. The incongruities were too immense for his mind to reconcile. This elderly prisoner, about to die, was offering to save the world. In any other context, the thought would have caused laughter. But while the interrogator didn't entirely understand what the Avatar meant about God, he picked up on the Avatar's sense of certainty, and he needed that feeling for himself.

Just as the Avatar had expected, a process of cognitive dissonance took hold of the interrogator's mind. His subconscious, a dormant giant, exerted control over his conscious, and its first order of business was ending the discomfort of confusion. And so it remapped the memories of the past few minutes, making the

Avatar seem more persuasive than he had been, causing the ideas that made no sense to the interrogator suddenly to seem right and obvious. The interrogator considered that this old man— bedraggled, unkempt, unarmed—had penetrated H2 outer defenses, so obviously he must have extraordinary capacity. This morsel of credibility expanded in the interrogator's head, connecting synapses that had dangled free, solving the dissonance, creating a new reality, new perception, new memories. The interrogator came to think that there *was* some chance that the Avatar understood the nature of God in a way that no one else did. What else was this old man capable of? Could he stop a war?

Thoughts collided in the interrogator's head, a mental clanging that hurt, and so his subconscious compensated in the only way it could, by adjusting his perception until he saw the Avatar as not a crazy old man but the savior of the world. This was the same process that all cult leaders used to control their flocks, but the Avatar had done it in minutes. And when the adjustment was done, for one brief moment, the interrogator felt something he had never felt before. It was intoxicating, transcending: He felt he mattered.

"You won't be forgotten," said the Avatar.

"I won't?" asked the interrogator.

"I'll tell Patrick what you did today," said the Avatar.

His words penetrated the interrogator and lifted him up in his chair. The interrogator felt the tug of a million years of evolution. Dormant instructions in his DNA activated: *Protect the family, protect the tribe, protect the species, follow the leader, and find meaning.* Then came the sudden flush of knowing, the realization, the certainty, and the peace.

An autopsy would later reveal that both shots were fired simultaneously. The I-Wing guard's lifeless body bounced off the wall while the interrogator staggered backwards, mortally wounded, landing in a pile against the table. No one would ever know why.

AVATAR MEETS GENERAL CRUZ

General Cruz's control center was in full operation. The wall monitors showed the satellite images of al-Zee's ground forces. The room was crackling with operational chatter, the sound of keyboards, rolling chairs, sliding bulletproof doors. Cruz was surrounded by several of his top officers on the promenade overlooking the control room.

"What's the status of the battle platform in the Indian Ocean?" asked Cruz.

"Seventy-five percent operational, sir," responded General Gallen, head of the Platform Battle Group.

"How long before we're a hundred percent?"

"Ten days. Maybe a week if we cut some corners," answered Gallen.

"How many troops do we have in the theater?" asked Cruz, looking at General Fuch.

"Seven hundred and fifty thousand on the ground. That includes fifty thousand Special Ops," Fuchs said.

Cruz took a deep breath and scanned the operational monitors, absorbing the readouts about enemy location, munitions, deployment, and likely losses from each attack scenario. On the most optimistic scenario, Cruz would lose fewer than 10,000 men. Worst case, 250,000. In every war game scenario the computers were cranking out, Cruz won. No price seemed too high, considering the stakes. The other side didn't fare so well. Their losses would be enormous.

"Gentlemen, tell me what day we ought to start this thing," said Cruz, still looking straight ahead.

"I recommend waiting at least a month" came a voice from behind Cruz.

"Waiting for what?" asked Cruz, displeased with the ambiguous response.

"Until you know what you're doing" came the answer.

Cruz whipped around, looking for the subordinate whose flippancy had just ended his military career. The general felt the rush of blood to his face—the one that he had felt so many times in combat, before squeezing the trigger and ending the mortal existence of an unlucky opponent. He was stunned at the sight of an old man with a plaid blanket standing behind him—an old man who should have been a grease spot under his limousine, or a dismantled corpse in I-Wing.

The lower-ranking generals formed a semicircle, just staring at the old man, not sure what to do. The Avatar's eyes locked on to Cruz's as if connected by wire. No one had looked at Cruz that way for a long, long time. For the first time in his life, the general was speechless.

"I'm sorry," offered the Avatar. "I guess your question wasn't directed at me."

The generals didn't know what to make of this situation. This was the most secure military location on the planet, which led them to think that anyone inside must have a good reason to be there, despite all outward appearance to the contrary. The generals were dumbfounded by the incongruity. There seemed no danger from the old man, so their fight-or-flight reflexes never kicked in. And when they tried to solve the puzzle with their rational facilities, all they got was brainlock. *The old man couldn't be standing there. But he was there. Therefore he must have a purpose.* Each of the generals concluded that someone else must know why he was there, and there had to be a good reason.

"Who are you?" demanded Cruz, drawing his sidearm and aiming between the Avatar's eyes.

Following Cruz's lead, the generals drew their sidearms too, none wanting to be the last to realize there was danger.

"Are you afraid of old blankets?" asked the Avatar, with a relaxed smile.

Cruz was not amused. "I understand that you know our battle plans. How do you know?" he demanded.

"I'd be happy to tell you, but it's a long story," answered the Avatar. "I get the impression that you're in a hurry."

"How did you get out of I-Wing alive?" barked Cruz.

"I'm rather pressed for time. Would you mind terribly if we got to the important matters first?"

"Such as?" growled Cruz, looking at the Avatar at the end of his pistol.

"Do you have an office where we can talk? Your generals aren't ready for what I have to tell you," said the Avatar.

"You'll talk right now, or I'll put a bullet in your skull," threatened Cruz.

"If I may be frank, in the interest of time, we both know you won't. You need to find out how I know of your battle plans. And I should think you'd like to know al-Zee's battle plans while you're in an inquisitive mood. You tried torturing me, and now you know that that didn't work. You're not the sort of man who tries a failed strategy twice. So now you'll try the next obvious strategy, which is to sit down and listen to me. That's who you are."

Cruz was furious at himself for not realizing the old man might know more than just the plans of the Christian Alliance, furious for somehow losing control of this situation to an old man, furious for being distracted from the task at hand, and furious at the weapon in his hand that was now utterly useless. He holstered his weapon and yelled to Lieutenant Waters to join them. The generals stood speechless as Cruz, the old man, and Waters exited the control room toward the High Commander's war room office.

"Waters," said Cruz, "if this old man does anything dangerous, shoot him. I'm not sure what we have here yet."

"Do you want me in the room?" asked Waters.

"Keep the door open, but wait outside," ordered Cruz.

The H2 Command office was designed for efficiency, not luxury. It stayed uninhabited except when Cruz needed to run things from there, which until now had only been drills. The desk and other surfaces were devoid of paperwork and personal effects.

"Sit down," Cruz said to the Avatar.

The Avatar walked to the large chair behind the command desk and sat down. Cruz watched with a combination of anger and amusement as he lost his seat to the old man. The general decided to stand, so at least he'd have a height advantage.

"Let's start with who you are," he said.

"My name is Avatar. Many years ago I was a package delivery-man in San Francisco. Now I just try to help wherever my particular skills are needed. That is why I'm here today."

"And what are your particular skills, other than spooking my entire staff, and escaping from a maximum-security interrogation center?" asked Cruz.

"I am immune from delusion," answered the Avatar.

"I have to wonder how often that comes in handy," scoffed Cruz.

"Take your current situation," explained the Avatar. "The world stands on the brink of losing two billion souls before the year is out. The stakes are enormous. Al-Zee's people believe they will go to paradise for killing their enemies. But you know they are deluded, do you not?"

"That's obvious," said Cruz.

"But it's not obvious to *them*," corrected the Avatar. "How do you explain to yourself their wrongness?"

"They've been brainwashed and they don't know it."

"So you agree that people who are brainwashed don't know it, even if someone helpful tries to point it out?" asked the Avatar.

"Pretty much," huffed Cruz, getting impatient with this line of conversation that didn't seem to be going anywhere.

"Then you understand that it's entirely possible that *you're* brainwashed into believing the Christian forces will prevail over the Muslims because God wants it so," said the Avatar.

"Maybe in theory, but I'm *not* brainwashed. The Muslims are deluded, and nothing is gonna stop them except death. I plan to answer their prayers," said Cruz.

"I'm confused by your answer," said the Avatar. "On the one hand you say you wouldn't know if you were brainwashed, and on the other hand you say you're sure you're not."

"Brainwashing isn't that common. What are the odds someone brainwashed not only me but everyone I work with?" asked Cruz.

"About the same as the odds that two billion Muslims would be brainwashed," said the Avatar.

"Okay, you made your little point. But none of it matters. I believe what I believe. The war is happening. God is on our side and we're going to win it."

"Surely you know you can't win it, don't you?" asked the Avatar.

"I've got a hundred-to-one advantage in firepower. This thing will be over in sixty days."

"Have you ever wondered why al-Zee hasn't used chemical or biological weapons for the past ten years?" asked the Avatar.

"His loons did a few gas attacks years ago and it cost them a lot in public opinion. Al-Zee is a smooth operator. He's running a PR campaign as much as a war of terror. He's not looking for big numbers of dead, just the most photogenic events. Hell, he's been recording his own bombings and e-mailing the recordings to the media for a decade. Lethal gas doesn't look exciting on television. Explosions do."

"That's partly right," agreed the Avatar. "But where do you think all the stockpiles of biological weapons went?"

"Probably to some cave in Syria. There are a million holes in the ground."

"Maybe this is a good time to tell you how I knew your war plans," offered the Avatar.

Footsteps ran up the hallway. A security officer handed a note to Waters outside the door. The note described the scene they had just discovered at I-Wing: two dead, door wide open. Waters looked into the room, deciding to say nothing for now, and put the note in his pocket before dismissing the guard.

"You see," explained the Avatar, "I asked myself what I would do if I had your military assets, your nearly pathological need to control your environment, and only an average level of awareness of your own delusions. Then I sorted through the news stories that speculated on your various possible plans, and focused initially on the ones that were obviously leaked by your own people."

"I'm going to ignore your description of me for a minute," said Cruz. "Tell me how you could tell which battle plans were leaks?"

"Those were the ones that gave away too much information and would allow an enemy to prepare," said the Avatar. "And they were the uncreative ideas. The leaks allowed me to eliminate many alternatives. From there I focused on the one best option for gaining your political and military objectives, the path with the greatest certainty."

"Clever bastard. But you're wrong. Completely wrong."

The Avatar smiled.

"I'm not talking about your *real* plan. I'm talking about your counterfeit plan—the one you sold to your own generals and to the Christian governments."

Cruz put on his best poker face. He didn't like the direction this was taking. No one else on Earth knew that his *real* plan was extermination. Never before had a general hidden his war plans from his own staff until the onset of war. How could the Avatar have guessed?

"Deducing your real plan was easier," answered the Avatar to the question that wasn't asked. "I simply imagined what I would do if I were you and wanted to be one hundred percent sure of permanent victory. And of course I ignored the impact on enemy civilian populations, as I know you will, since you believe that your own civilian population is at risk if you lose."

Cruz stayed quiet, trying to reveal nothing with his look or his tone of voice. His silence was an invitation to elaborate.

"Your plan is extermination," said the Avatar.

The word hit Cruz like an electrical shock. It was his private word—the one he used only in his thoughts.

"First your armies will knock out communication in the war zones. The media will be banned. And then you will systematically annihilate the civilian and military populations."

Cruz needed to change the direction of the conversation. The Avatar's predictions were rocking his confidence. Was it that easy to guess his moves? If so, did al-Zee already know? Then it hit him. "That's enough about me. Tell me what al-Zee plans to do after we attack. If you're so smart, you must know."

"As we speak, al-Zee's sleeper cells have moved massive amounts of biological weapons into every major American and European metropolitan area. They're operating independently now, having already received instructions that when your bombers make their first run, they'll unleash their weapons, destroying much of Western civilization in less than a week."

Cruz's face went pale. That wasn't even a scenario his planners had considered. The long absence of chemical and biological attacks had made everyone believe that that sort of thing was behind them. "If al-Zee has that capability, why wouldn't he have used it already, or at least threatened to use it?" asked Cruz.

"Al-Zee understands that a few bombings a week are good for morale on his side. But a massive biological attack on the West would bring certain annihilation to his people, his family, and himself. He's saving the final move until there's no other option. He's betting that your army will stop cold when your people realize their homelands have been decimated. And if he stops you in your tracks, with your one-hundred-to-one advantage in fire-power, as you say, his prestige and power will reach new highs. He will become a superpower overnight."

Outside the door, Waters strained to hear every word. He was mesmerized, but unlike Cruz, he was not worried. Waters didn't have the capacity for worrying.

The Avatar continued, "Humanity is like a huge organic computer. The hardware is functioning fine—reproducing more humans, creating food, learning—but the software is broken. Beliefs are our software. When the software works properly, our beliefs help us survive. Sometimes there are glitches in the software, in the form of delusions that are harmful. My job is to remove the glitches."

"What can one old man do to change the minds of every person on the planet?" Cruz challenged.

"I only need to change one mind," said the Avatar.

"If you mean me, you're too late. I'm not changing my battle plans because of your nutty predictions," said Cruz.

"No, all I need from you is some extra time. I have introduced some doubt into your plan, and now you will try to find out if I'm right. You will delay your battle until you can check out my version of al-Zee's plans. And that is all I ask of you."

Cruz sat down in a small visitor's chair. Somehow this old man had indeed done what he said he would do. He had introduced doubt. And it would make Cruz pause. He would send out his spooks and Special Forces and try to find out if there was any way the Avatar's guess about al-Zee was right. Cruz was angry, but that feeling was starting to seem normal.

"How do you plan to change the minds of a billion people?" asked Cruz.

"It's several billion, actually," corrected the Avatar.

"Same question."

"Everything that humans create is in their own image, in some way. The purest example is the computer. Even in the early days, computers had memory, as people do, and they could do math. Now computers have been programmed to think, play chess, create art, hear, see, touch, and hold conversations. More to my point, every computer, no matter its purpose, has a reboot switch for when the software gets locked up. One button."

"You plan to reboot several billion people?" asked Cruz.

"I have to find the one person who is the equivalent of the reboot button," answered the Avatar.

"I'm the closest thing you're going to find," said Cruz.

"No, I'm looking for the one who has the most influence on people's thoughts, and that person is unlikely to be a world leader. Everyone has at least one influencer in his life, someone who can change your mind simply by expressing an opinion that is different from your own. And that influencer in turn is influenced by at least one other person, and so on. This vast web of influence connects every person, including the dead, but we're unaware of its reach and extent. We know of our immediate influencers, and nothing more."

"You're saying there's one person on Earth who can change the mind of everyone else on Earth?" asked Cruz.

"Yes. And that person is probably not aware of it," said the Avatar.

"How do you know such a person exists?" asked Cruz.

"The universe has favored patterns," said the Avatar. "You need only look at what people build to know how humans are designed. Every computer has a reboot button. Of all the things humans have built, computers are the most like us. And so it follows that somewhere there is a human reboot button, one person whose opinion can reset the opinions of all of humanity."

"You know that I can't let you leave, don't you? If half of what you said is right, you're too valuable to risk capture by al-Zee's men. And even if what you say *isn't* right, you've been to I-Wing. I can't let you leave."

"What I know is that you will escort me to the front gate. And sometime in the next few weeks, when I need your help, you will give it," said the Avatar, standing to leave.

"What makes you so sure?" asked Cruz.

"I've studied your biography. You played chess at the Grand Master level when you were ten. You developed your tough side as a defense against the other children, especially the older ones, who considered your chess skills a topic for ridicule," said the Avatar.

"You didn't find that in any biography," challenged Cruz, who knew every word that had ever been published about him.

"I read about your chess skills. The rest is a familiar pattern. But to your earlier point, you are a man who understands strategy and risk. That's why you are where you are today. You listened to my story and judged the odds of it being true to be somewhere in the range of one percent. And you did an expected value calculation, multiplying the number of people who might die in the war by one percent, and set that aside as the number of people whose lives hang in the balance, statistically speaking. And being rational, you are now deciding that letting me continue my journey is worth the risk."

"You're clever, that's for sure. But you have no idea what al-Zee's thugs could do to you if they caught you," said Cruz.

"Lieutenant Waters knows," said the Avatar.

Cruz turned toward the door and looked at Waters standing just outside. Waters reached into his pocket and took out the note. Cruz extended his hand in a silent command. Waters complied. Cruz read the note describing the dead interrogator and the dead guard at I-Wing. He looked at the Avatar, folded the note, and put it in his pocket.

"Follow me," Cruz said, as he turned to exit.

Cruz passed by Waters at the door. The Avatar stopped and looked at Waters, peering deeply into the lieutenant's unyielding eyes. Anyone else would have been unnerved. Waters just looked back.

"We'll talk again," said the Avatar, before following Cruz to the stairwell, through the guarded lobby, out the security perimeter, and through the main gate.

GLOBAL INFORMATION
CORPORATION

The Avatar walked a half mile to the nearest hydrocab taxi sensor and stood on it. For the past five years, taxis had been the only form of four-wheel street travel, all Fords, all hydrogen engines. When al-Zee's forces started bombing the United States and Europe on a weekly basis, it became unthinkably unpatriotic to drive a gas-guzzling car. Soon, it became unpatriotic to own *any* car. The Green Party had become a major social force, arguing successfully that every time you filled the tank of your SUV, you paid al-Zee to bomb your neighbor.

The last holdouts, mostly the rich and the cynical, were converted when American ultranationalists took matters into their own hands and started dynamiting domestic automobile factories. Of the American carmakers, only Ford survived those years, barely, thanks to government loans and a promise to make nothing but hydrogen taxis.

The taxi sensor below the Avatar's feet sensed his weight, registered two points of pressure, and relayed the information "one passenger" to the global taxi satellite system, which broadcast it back to Earth along with geographic coordinates. It wasn't possible for most people to call a taxi using their phones, or indeed to call anyone who wasn't a business associate or family member. To fight terrorists, the phone network was programmed to allow only authorized calls. Every citizen was required to submit a list of friends and business associates to the Department of Communications. Only those calls were allowed.

Three taxis were available and nearby; they snapped their engines into drive at the first indication on their navigation screens that a potential passenger waited nearby. Hydrocab profit margins were kept artificially low by the government, so only the most aggressive operators survived.

The first hydrocab screeched around the corner and came to a noisy stop in front of the Avatar, just as the second and third appeared a block away. The Avatar leaned down and examined the driver, an unpleasant-looking fellow named Arun Singh, according to his operating license, which was prominently displayed. The Avatar smiled and motioned to the driver to continue on without him. Singh snarled but didn't wait around to argue, burning his tires in disgust. He had become accustomed to older customers waving him on because they mistook him for a Muslim. He hated this country lately, but it was not his day to change it.

The second hydrocab saw the opportunity and pulled up. The Avatar smiled to the driver, a woman in her fifties named Noriko Yamamoto. She returned a dead stare, expecting him to get in. The Avatar waved her off. Her blank look became anger as the cab pulled away.

The third cab approached and the Avatar looked inside. The driver's license said Hector Rodriguez. Hector was a young man, early thirties, with dark friendly eyes and a well-manicured mustache. He was smiling. The Avatar opened the back door and got in.

"Destination?" mumbled the driver.

"Do you know where the GIC headquarters building is?" asked the Avatar, referring to Global Information Corporation, a household name by now.

"Sí."

As they drove, the Avatar felt a pattern forming. He remembered a time before he became Avatar, when patterns were largely invisible to him. But after years of practice, he had developed an additional sense, finely tuned to pattern recognition. Often the patterns aborted before becoming fully formed, evaporating as false signals, reverting back to chaos and waiting for the next energy surge. Today the Avatar noticed the spring weather, seventy-two degrees Fahrenheit according to the weather display in the hydrocab. No wind, perfect for being outdoors after several days of rain. He remembered the radio that was playing when he first visited Cruz's headquarters; it was tuned to a baseball game. It was four o'clock now, only a few more hours of natural light. School was out. Baseball was in the air. The Avatar noticed the homes in the neighborhood as they passed, the price range entirely appropriate to young families with children. In this economy, most minors were unsupervised while their parents worked. Senior citizens, most of them retired without savings, lived in special economical housing zones too far from where the kids lived to be useful babysitters. The older children babysat for the entire block, and they had their own agendas, with attentiveness near the bottom.

"I might tell you to stop quickly. Will you do that for me?" asked the Avatar.

"Sí," said the driver.

"I don't mean when we get to GIC. I mean in the middle of the street, and you won't have much warning. I will compensate you well if you do as I ask."

"Sí," said the driver.

The Avatar cracked open his window, listening to the sounds of spring, the commotion of air around the cab, the tires on pavement. He heard the distinctive and nearly ubiquitous sounds of distant hydrocab horns, an occasional bird, and then the sound of young laughter, boys shouting, joking, and playing. The patterns always started incomplete, waiting until somehow his subconscious filled in the important pieces. It was like a musician who knows the next note but doesn't know how he knows, or the math prodigy who knows the answer to the equation without being conscious of doing the calculation. The Avatar had developed this skill as a side effect of reaching the fifth and highest level of consciousness, a place that he alone inhabited.

"Stop now," ordered the Avatar.

Hector glanced briefly in his rearview mirror, first to see if anyone was following him too closely, second to see the eyes of the old man. Then he hit the brakes, hard. He waited a beat, expecting the explanation, and it came, indirectly, in the form of a ten-year-old boy darting out from behind a shrub, running directly into the path of the cab, chasing a baseball, in what could have been his last moments of life. The boy looked up just in time to see the hydrocab, scaring him witless before he realized it was at a full stop. The boy let the ball continue. He stood bolt upright and looked into the hydrocab, and into the eyes of the Avatar. The Avatar smiled, partly in amusement at the boy's reaction, partly out of smugness for having identified a particularly subtle pattern before it formed.

Hector was stiff, his eyes wide as saucers. He looked at the old man by mirror, unable to blink.

"You may continue," said the Avatar, as the boy stepped to the curb, still shaking.

One day the boy would be a surgeon, pioneering a procedure for partial spinal replacement. During every operation, as his hands expertly worked his patient's central nervous system, saving a life that would otherwise be lost, the surgeon would always remember this day, and the eyes of the Avatar. And he would wonder how the hydrocab had known to stop. It would be the greatest puzzle of his life.

The hydrocab stopped in front of the GIC world headquarters building, a modest complex only four stories high. A consortium of countries had created GIC ten years ago to pool databases from all available sources. The countries passed laws making it illegal to have any sort of commercial information system that didn't feed into GIC every evening. The idea was that terrorist sleeper cells could be identified by their activities once all databases were merged. Special mining software searched unimaginable mounds of digital data every minute looking for clues, such as purchases of materials that might be made into weapons, access to terror-related web sites, even hydrocab travel in the vicinity of suspected targets.

When GIC was first proposed, concerned citizens rioted to stop it. People saw it as a threat to freedom, something that could easily become worse than the violence it sought to eliminate. The resistance ended when al-Zee's operatives started bombing anti-GIC rallies. The protesters made wonderful targets because lots of camera crews were there to record the carnage. Al-Zee was called a terrorist, but he was also a brilliant tactician who knew the value of free publicity. And he wasn't worried about GIC. He figured that an organization that large, run by a coalition of a hundred governments, had no chance of being effective.

He would have been right, but he didn't count on the bureaucratic logjam having the ironic effect of totally freeing the programmers and techies to do what they needed to do. And budgets were no problem either because terror-defense was a world priority. Global Information Corporation was so poorly managed that the technical people started forming self-managed groups, operating without approval, and actually finished the majority of the design and implementation before the governing bodies agreed on a mission statement. It was one of the greatest technical achievements of all time, completed astonishingly quickly, thanks to an utter lack of management and the skill of one particular technical genius.

The Avatar waved his universal payment card over the console in the backseat, pressed the button marked "50% tip," and hit Enter.

"I will be about an hour. Wait here for me," said the Avatar.

Hector turned and looked at him, surprised by a request that sounded more like a command. It was inappropriate to ask a hydrocab to wait five minutes, much less an hour. There were plenty of hydrocabs in the area, and if Hector waited, he'd lose an hour's worth of fares.

"I know," said the Avatar, responding to the expression on Hector's face. "It's wrong to ask you to wait. But you will wait, won't you?"

"Sí," said Hector, more confused than annoyed.

The Avatar, still looking like a bum with a plaid blanket, approached the guard's desk in the lobby of GIC. The guard gave a look of practiced indifference, the sort that says, "I might be working as a security guard, but you're not better than me."

"I'm here to see your director of human resources," said the Avatar with a pleasant smile.

"Name?" asked the guard, without making eye contact.

"Avatar."

"I don't see you on the list. Do you have an appointment with Mr. Portius?"

"I'm meeting with him in five minutes," said the Avatar.

"Someone forgot to call your name down. I always tell them that they have to call the name down at least an hour ahead of time. But they have so much turnover up there, no one knows their head from their elbow."

"Perhaps you could add my name to the list," suggested the Avatar.

The security guard made eye contact with the Avatar for the first time, and saw what he thought might be the most harmless looking human on the planet.

"That would be a security violation."

"Yes, but you wouldn't want to disappoint Mr. Portius."

"I'm between a rock and a wet spot here. I'd better call up and see what his office says," grumbled the guard, reaching for his phone.

Jennifer answered the phone on the fifth ring, after remembering that Portius' secretary was out to lunch, leaving her to cover the phones.

"John Portius' office. This is Jennifer. How may I help you?"

"This is Frank, in the lobby. I got a guy here to see Mr. Portius and he isn't on the list."

"What's his name?" asked Jennifer helpfully, having nothing to compare against the answer, but feeling it was the responsible question to ask.

"Avatar."

"Hmm," stalled Jennifer, not wanting to admit she didn't have access to Portius' calendar and so it was silly to have asked for his name. "Yes, that sounds right," she bluffed.

"Thanks. I'll send him up," said the guard.

"Fifth floor. Sign in first. Here's your name tag."

"Thank you. I guess it was a good choice for me to come here at lunchtime," said the Avatar without explanation.

The guard half-listened, filled out the temporary security badge, and replied, "Yeah. I'm hungry too. Put this tag on your shirt."

John Portius was surprised to see the Avatar standing in his office. The old man obviously wasn't an employee because the company routinely weeded out any workers over fifty. The man wasn't a vendor, because they always dressed better than the employees. He had to be there for *some* reason. The temporary security badge advertised that he wasn't dangerous.

"Can I help you?" asked Portius.

"Yes," replied the Avatar.

"Um . . . how?" asked Portius, shifting uncomfortably in his chair.

"I would like to speak with your most angry employee," said the Avatar.

"Do I know you?"

"I hear that question a lot, and no, you don't," said the Avatar.

"Who are you? And why do you want to talk to an angry employee?"

"My name is Avatar. The rest would take too long to explain. But I can assure you it's a fascinating reason. And I don't want *any* angry employee. I want the *angriest.*"

"Well, I'm sorry, Mr. Avatar, but I'm very busy today. I don't believe you have an appointment."

"That's okay. I'll just stand outside your office," said the Avatar.

"I'd rather you didn't," said Portius, reaching for a ringing phone.

The Avatar left the office and stood just out of sight, while Portius' attention went to the phone call and another crisis in full bloom. The Avatar smiled politely as employees walked past, none of them quite sure what to make of him. Forty minutes later, a walking tornado turned the corner and headed straight at him, spewing a monologue of antimanagement invectives. He was wiry, about six feet tall, with unkempt black hair and a walk that looked more praying mantis than programmer. He was bare-footed, a violation of several corporate rules.

"This entire place is filled with idiots! Who's doing the hiring here? Do you just have to say you *want* to be a programmer and that's good enough?" asked Eric Mackey of anyone who might be within earshot. The Avatar watched as a manager on the way out of his office thought better of it and did a quick U-turn to avoid the approaching wrath.

Mackey liked to mark his territory with indignant yelling. He liked attention, he liked being right, and he liked it even better when other people could be proven wrong. He was a bona fide technical genius, a human patent factory, and a recipe for social disaster. But Mackey didn't wait for disasters to find him; he sought them with the delight of a hunter on opening day of deer season. He found guilty pleasure in exposing the mental foibles of those less gifted, and that included almost everyone.

The Avatar could sense Mackey's pattern, clean and unmistakable. He was the angriest employee and, by extension, the most talented, because anyone with lesser value would have been fired for that sort of behavior. "What took you so long?" asked the Avatar, verbally intercepting Mackey, who was on a mission to dress down the director of human resources.

Mackey stopped and sized up the Avatar, instantly recognizing him as a puzzle. Mackey liked puzzles even more than he liked yelling at people who annoyed him. This would be worth a few minutes of his time. Then he could get back to the main attraction—yelling at idiots.

"What do you mean?" asked Mackey, requesting the next clue.

"There's something you don't know about your databases," said the Avatar.

Mackey scrunched his face and stared at the Avatar. If there was one thing he hated, it was the prospect that someone knew something he didn't. This old man might be a nut, but it didn't matter where the challenge was coming from. A challenge was a challenge.

"I highly doubt that, buddy," he said.

"Very well then. Continue with what you were doing," said the Avatar.

Mackey hesitated, took a step toward Portius' office, then stopped and turned back.

"What don't I know?" he asked.

"It might take some time to explain. If you're in a hurry I can wait until after you've yelled at Mr. Portius."

"Ah, it'll hold. I yell at him every day. Come here," said Mackey, starting off toward an empty conference room across the hall. The Avatar followed. Inside, Mackey swung a chair from the table and pushed it toward the Avatar, an invitation to sit. Mackey took the nice chair at the head of the table.

"Let's hear it. I've got two minutes," he said.

Mackey never thought to ask the Avatar his name, or what he was doing in the building dressed like a bum. None of that seemed important to Mackey. He just wanted to know if there really was a hole in his knowledge of the database, as unlikely as that seemed to him.

"Your organization holds the data of every transaction in the modern world," said the Avatar.

"So far, you've proven that you know what building you're in. Does this get better?" asked Mackey, pleased with his put-down.

"You know what people buy, what Internet pages they read, where they travel, what they like, and what they don't like. To date, you have only used that information in the way that your charter has authorized you: searching for terrorists."

"I am getting seriously bored now," said Mackey, leaning back in his chair.

"The data holds more than you imagined. There are patterns you haven't mined, that you never thought to seek. Those patterns are the most important part of the data, lying dormant, waiting to be discovered."

"No," said Mackey. "Our data mining software finds all the important patterns. I wrote most of that code myself."

The Avatar stood and walked to the whiteboard, picked up an erasable pen, and started to draw concentric circles.

"We think our preferences are caused by our reason. Sometimes we think our preferences are caused by biology, or experience. Those are all parts of the answer, but only small parts. For every decision we make, there is always someone who influenced it, either currently or in the past. Usually, people are unaware of who influences them. Sometimes it's as simple as a group of friends who all dress alike, not noticing that one of them always starts the trend. It is our most basic nature to imitate other people. The mimicry is most obvious with babies, but it never stops. We don't notice our own copying because we're so adept at rationalizing what we do, even to ourselves. Sometimes our role models are people we don't even know. When President Kennedy stopped wearing hats in the early 1960s, the entire men's hat industry crumbled. If you asked anyone why he stopped wearing a hat, he would give you a reason that sounded plausible without ever realizing what the real influence was."

This was getting a little more interesting, Mackey thought. He didn't know where it was heading, and he liked that. The Avatar continued, illustrating his point on the board as he talked. "Your database captures these lines of influence, but only indirectly. Every trend, every new idea, every innovation, every opinion, starts with one person and ripples outward, changing direction, sparking new trends, covering its tracks, until no one really knows its origin."

"Okay. So, I can use my database to find out who was the first person to eat lemon-buffalo dessert. What's so exciting about that?"

The Avatar put down the marker and turned to look at Mackey. "This war—the one that is about to happen—do you know why?" he asked.

"Everyone knows why. The frickin' Muslims are killing us. We have to kill them before they kill us," said Mackey, echoing the popular notion of the Christian Alliance.

"Why are they killing you?" asked the Avatar.

"Because they're jealous of our freedom. We have so much and they have squat. I'd be pissed too if I were them."

"Since when do people kill out of envy?" asked the Avatar. "Is this something new?"

"I admit I can't think of any good examples from history. Usually some dictator is just trying to grab more power. But I don't think the Muslims want power. I think they just want to whack us because they like it. Or it's their religion. Or they've been brainwashed or something."

"My point is that you thought you knew the answer to the most important question in the history of humanity—why the war will happen—but now you are not so sure."

"It's self-defense," tried Mackey. "Their leader is crazy."

"Have you ever noticed that every leader who opposes your country is 'crazy'? Doesn't that seem like a big coincidence?"

"Yeah, I kind of wonder about that," agreed Mackey.

"And do you realize that the Muslims believe *our* leaders are crazy?"

"I guess they would."

"The collective world opinions that are pushing us toward war are an idea virus. The virus has spread and mutated over the years until no one knows how it started. No one understands the real reasons for the war," said the Avatar.

"And you *do*?" asked Mackey, sarcastically.

"There is no reason. Society has become like a computer that's stuck in a loop. It needs to be rebooted. It needs a new program. And that is why I am here," said the Avatar.

"You want to reprogram humanity?" asked Mackey, trying to suppress a smile.

"Hiding in your database, several layers deep, is a path of influence that leads to one person. That person is, in effect, the reboot key. We need only change the opinion of that one person, and the rest will happen automatically, though no one will notice the source of the change."

"Well, that's a nice fairy tale. But I don't believe that that one person exists. Who do you think it is, a politician or celebrity of some sort?"

"It could be anyone," said the Avatar. "The problem is that it's impossible to write a program so sophisticated that it could filter out the noise in the data and find the underlying connections. It simply can't be done."

Mackey's eyes lit up like flares. He hated to be told something couldn't be done. He hated it, hated it, and hated it. Granted, he couldn't immediately see how such a thing could be done, and he didn't believe these lines of influence were all the Avatar said they were, but he sure as hell could write a program to find out if a primary influencer existed, given enough time.

The Avatar stood to leave. "I must be going now," he said. "I appreciate your time."

"That's it?" asked Mackey.

"Yes. I'm done here for now. But I'll be back in a week."

"Back for what?"

The Avatar just looked at Mackey. It was a look that said, *You know what I mean, and I know you know.* The Avatar was down the hall, around the corner, and waiting for the elevator when he heard Mackey shouting at the top of his lungs, still in the conference room.

"It's *not* impossible. You bastard!"

The Avatar allowed a smile as he walked into the elevator. A woman from auditing was the lone occupant. She saw the Avatar's smile and mirrored it. It had been a hideous day for her, capping a hideous week, but suddenly she felt safe and happy. The feeling lasted the entire ride to the lobby, and several hours more, until she saw her first angry frown coming down the hallway in the other direction. She frowned for the rest of the day.

HECTOR'S
TERRORIST CELL

Hector was waiting in his hydrocab. He'd endured a string of taunts from the other hydrocab drivers working in the area. Only suckers waited for a fare to do his business and return. First, it was dead time, and you never knew how long it would be. Sometimes the customer never returned at all. Second, the streets were covered with available hydrocabs, so waiting made no sense at all. To the other drivers, this was a sign of someone who either was new to the game or had no backbone. Either way, they found amusement in his idleness.

The Avatar got in the cab and thanked Hector for waiting. Hector just sighed and nodded. "Destination?" he asked in a low mumble.

"Take me to your boss," the Avatar said.

Hector's eyes drilled into the rearview mirror, trying to assess the meaning of this request. The Avatar expected no immediate verbal response. He was looking for confirmation of a pattern he'd seen developing when he first hailed the hydrocab.

"I don't mean your taxi boss," said the Avatar. "You can stop pretending to be Hector the Mexican who only knows how to say 'sí.' You work for al-Zee. I would like you to take me to him."

Hector—actually Ali—reached under the seat and took out a handgun, making sure the Avatar saw it.

"How do you know this, old man?" Ali asked, no longer hiding an Arabic accent.

"I assume that al-Zee is monitoring the comings and goings at the major military sites, looking for intelligence. The hydrocabs operate outside the security perimeter, and there are so many of them they draw no attention. And most of the drivers are dark-skinned men, so you wouldn't draw attention."

"I mean how did you know that *I* was the one?" Ali said, miffed that his cover was so easily penetrated.

"You fit the profile—male, mid-thirties, dark skin. And you were the only one who tried to look friendly. No hydrocab driver tries to be friendly," said the Avatar.

Ali smiled at his gaffe. It was only obvious after the Avatar said it.

"You guessed just from that?" asked Ali.

"Well, I should also tell you, in case you plan to stay on this assignment, that even a Mexican who has only been in this country for ten minutes knows how to say 'yes' in English. The 'sí señor' business was over the top."

"I did *not* say *señor,*" Ali protested.

"And when you waited for me at GIC, well, that was just plain clumsy terrorism," said the Avatar.

"Okay, okay. I get the picture. Now *you* get the picture," said Ali angrily, pointing his gun at the Avatar. "Tell me who you are and why you were at Cruz's headquarters."

"My name is Avatar. I was revealing al-Zee's war plans to General Cruz."

"How would you know our war plans?" asked Ali, looking around to make sure passersby didn't see his gun.

"In the interest of time, if it's not terribly impolite, would it be okay if we skipped this conversation and you took me directly to your nearest torture center?" asked the Avatar.

"I'm the one with the gun. We'll do what I say we'll do," said Ali.

"That's not exactly true. By now you've figured out that you can't shoot me here. And the best place to kill me, after torturing me, of course, is wherever you normally do that sort of thing. So we'll be leaving for there I would think."

Ali paused to let that sink in, while trying to look menacing. There was a compelling logic to what the old man said. "If you try to get out, I'll shoot you, old man," he said, trying to regain control of the situation.

"Were you listening to any of this conversation?" the Avatar asked with evident amusement.

Ali huffed and put the gun back under the seat. He stared at the Avatar in the mirror and started the engine.

"But first I think you should take me someplace out of sight and put a blindfold on me," said the Avatar.

Ali was fuming. That was exactly what he planned to do, but somehow it ruined the idea to hear it from the Avatar first.

"I think it's in the glove compartment," said the Avatar helpfully.

Ali shook his head in disgust, then opened the glove compartment, removed the ski cap, and tossed it into the backseat. The Avatar placed the cap on his head and pulled it down over his eyes.

"If I doze off, could you wake me when we're there?" he asked.

"Yes," agreed Ali, completely deflated.

The ski cap blocked the Avatar's vision, but his other senses fed a constant stream of information to his consciousness, where patterns formed, drawing a picture of his surroundings every bit as vivid as if he were viewing them in a book. He knew they were passing through Chinatown, judging from the stop-and-go traffic, the spices in the air, and the chatter on the sidewalk. Their speed picked up, and the road sounds began to reflect back to them, a clear indication they were in a tunnel. When the echoes stopped, the car turned left and accelerated. On the right came sounds of a public park, and beyond that, a tugboat exercised its horn. The air was a few degrees cooler already, a sign they were heading toward the ocean. They continued straight for several minutes, until sounds no longer reflected off nearby buildings on one side. They were at the shore, then turning into a driveway, over a noisy metal grate, and down a narrow alley.

Two large men took the Avatar by either arm and dragged him into a home. When his cap was removed, he was standing in the living room of a modest two-story stucco home. Ali was whispering to a round-faced, mustached man, who was clearly in charge of the local operation. The round-faced man listened and stared at the Avatar. The Avatar smiled, and waited his turn to talk.

"You claim to know al-Zee's plans?" the round-faced man asked.

"Yes. But the problem I see here is that *you* don't know his plans, so you have no way of knowing if I'm telling the truth. You wouldn't have any knowledge of the larger plan."

"Who are you?" the cell leader asked, already in a bad mood.

"My name is Avatar. I used to deliver packages."

"Do you think this is funny?" asked the cell leader. "You're looking at two choices today. Either you tell me what I want, and I kill you fast, or you make me hurt you. Which will it be?"

"I'd like the choice where I tell you what you want to know and then Ali drives me to the airport. I need to see al-Zee sometime in the next day or so. I'm hoping you can make that happen."

"Maybe some pain will make you talk some sense," snarled the cell leader.

"I think he *wants* to talk," said Ali, trying to help.

"Maybe your questions aren't good," offered one of the armed guards.

The cell leader swiped the contents of the coffee table onto the floor in a show of anger, making more of a cleaning problem than a point. He stood to look more menacing.

"Okay, old man, tell me what your game is. What were you doing at Cruz's headquarters?"

"I was telling him al-Zee's battle plans," explained the Avatar.

"And how would you know his battle plans? Is that something you learned from delivering packages?" The cell leader sneered.

"In a way," answered the Avatar, walking to a comfortable chair and sitting. "It's a matter of understanding probability." The cell leader wasn't expecting his prisoner to make himself at home. It happened so naturally that the Avatar was already happily seated before anyone could think to stop him. He began. "There are two impulses in every mind. One is the recognition of probability. It's the part of your brain that knows that the risk of dying in a plane crash, for example, is very low. The other impulse is your irrational mind, or your heart if you prefer the poetic label. That's the impulse that makes many people afraid of flying in spite of its relative safety."

"Your point?" growled the cell leader.

"Most people are trained from childhood to favor their irrational impulses when it comes to the most important questions in life. For example, you know how many religions there are in the world and therefore how unlikely it is for any one person, such as yourself, to have chosen the correct one. Yet you choose to ignore the odds. And that learned preference for ignoring statistics frames all of your thinking, sometimes obscuring the obvious."

"Okay, old man. This is fascinating, but now I want you to tell me how you know al-Zee's plans."

"I know al-Zee's plans because I understand the power of probability for explaining reality, whereas you, like most people, choose to ignore it. I assigned a probability to each of al-Zee's alternatives and realized that only one has a good chance of preserving his life and providing victory. Al-Zee is sure to come to the same choice," said the Avatar.

"And what choice is that?" asked the cell leader, visibly angry.

"Each of his cells—and that includes you—has large supplies of biological weapons, smuggled into the country in the past ten years. When Cruz attacks the Middle East, and al-Zee's forces are no match for the Christian Alliance, he will order you to unleash your weapons and annihilate life in all the major metropolitan centers of Cruz's homeland, at the rate of one city per day, maybe more. Then he will offer a truce to Cruz if he pulls back his forces. Al–Zee believes that Cruz will be persuaded by public opinion in his homeland to accept the peace offer. Al–Zee is mistaken, but nonetheless, that is his plan, because it has the best chance of succeeding, and al–Zee is a skilled tactician. If it doesn't work, al–Zee will stay in his underground fortress until everything aboveground is dead, emerging as the only viable power."

The cell leader stared at the Avatar. He had no way of knowing if the other cells had biological weapons, but the basement of *his* house *was* full of lethal drums. He made a conscious effort to send no confirming signals with his face.

"Wrong," said the cell leader. "Al–Zee's people have no weapons of mass destruction."

"You operate as a cell, do you not?" asked the Avatar.

"You already know that."

"Cells operate independently, with no knowledge of the others. You have no way of knowing whether the other cells have chemical or biological weapons. If you were telling the truth, you would have personalized your answer. You would have said you didn't know about the other cells. You would have said that *you* certainly don't have any of those weapons in your basement."

"I didn't say anything about the basement."

"Your assistant looked at the basement door when I mentioned biological weapons. That's probably the sort of thing you should discuss at your next staff meeting," said the Avatar, with a grin.

The cell leader, his two guards, and Ali all tried to look straight ahead, to conceal how right the Avatar was. They tried to look angry, which was easy, because they were hopping mad.

"I'll need to see al-Zee soon. Tomorrow would be good for me. Can you arrange that?" asked the Avatar.

"Why would al-Zee want to meet with you?" asked the cell leader.

"Because I know General Cruz's battle plans too," answered the Avatar. "It would take you forty-eight hours to torture the information out of me, or you can get it in twenty-four hours by helping me tell it to al-Zee directly. You think you have choices, but in fact, you have none," he explained.

The Avatar's argument made perfect sense to the cell leader, much to his annoyance. Somehow the round-faced man had completely lost control of this situation, if he ever had it.

On the way to the airport, Ali tried to avoid talking to the Avatar, but eventually the urge won.

"How do you do that?" he asked.

"Do what?"

"Know things," said Ali.

"Oh, that," said the Avatar.

"You knew what I meant before I clarified it, didn't you?" said Ali.

"Yes, but it seemed polite to let you complete the question," said the Avatar.

"So how do you do it?"

"Our ride isn't long enough to explain everything. But I will tell you in a general way, if you don't mind."

"Okay," said Ali.

"You see, the universe uses the same patterns over and over. The trick is to recognize the patterns," said the Avatar.

"How do you recognize patterns?"

"Partly by asking yourself questions. If you ask the right questions, the patterns present themselves."

"Can you teach me how to do that?" asked Ali.

"Not in our brief time together, but I will give you an example. Ask yourself this: Why do your leaders have bodyguards around them at all times?"

"To protect them from enemies, so they can fight for our people," said Ali. "Leaders are no good to us if they are dead."

"Don't you believe that God alone decides when your leaders will die?"

"Of course."

"So if only God decides when they die, that means that all human enemies are harmless until God determines otherwise?"

"Yes."

"Do you think your leaders know that?"

"Of course."

"Then the only explanation for the bodyguards is that they have been hired to protect the leaders from God himself, since God is their only known threat."

Ali just drove.

"What sort of person would hire bodyguards to protect him from God?" asked the Avatar.

Ali ignored the question.

"You don't need to answer," said the Avatar. "You know that either your leaders don't believe what they say they believe or they are irrational. Neither possibility is comforting on the eve of war."

Ali didn't speak for the rest of the trip. Several counterarguments came to mind, only to be rejected before they reached his mouth. The cab pulled up to the airport's loading zone. The Avatar thanked Ali for the ride. Ali just stared straight ahead, both hands on the steering wheel.

Inside the terminal, the Avatar studied the destination information for all the flights, looking for patterns. As he read the name of each city, all the memories of that city activated in his mind, forming patterns, with special attention to any news reports in the past five years.

The Avatar's mind cycled through unrelated facts about each city, feeling for patterns: *distances . . . number of terrorist attacks . . . counterterrorism arrests . . . friendly governments . . . arms dealers . . . terrain . . . news accounts . . . economies . . . religious extremism . . .*

The Avatar considered all of those patterns and more, scanning each city, pausing to meditate on what bubbled to the top: Cairo . . . Tehran . . . Riyadh . . . Qadum. There it was: Qadum, a city that didn't show up on any map five years ago. Now it had an international airport. It was a center of commerce for the Arab world. It was a city where huge amounts of construction would go unnoticed amid the other huge amounts of construction. It was a place where a world leader could start from scratch and build his underground fortress, escape tunnels, and defenses without being noticed. The Avatar bought a ticket for Qadum and waited at the gate.

AVATAR FLIES
TO QADUM

The Avatar settled into his business-class seat, collecting suspicious glances from the other travelers who noticed his ragged clothing. A forty-year-old banker arranged himself in the next seat, attending to his little pillow and his carry-on luggage, and handing his jacket to the flight attendant while ordering a Jack Daniel's on the rocks. He was a big man, Boston grown, Ivy League education. A glance at the Avatar and his ragged clothes convinced the banker that it might be a long flight.

A French auto executive, early fifties, dropped his briefcase and newspaper in the seat next to the banker, hunted for some overhead storage, and handed his jacket to a flight attendant. As the plane taxied down the runway, the Avatar meditated while the banker and the auto executive sipped their drinks. The Frenchman harrumphed at the front page of the paper, hoping to engage the banker and ultimately enrich the world with the magic and beauty of his opinions, but the banker wasn't having it.

"Stupid war," said the Frenchman, trying harder to engage the banker.

"No one wins," said the banker, trying to end the conversation with a comment that offered no traction.

"You know why we're heading to war, don't you?" the Frenchman asked.

The banker turned and looked at him, saying nothing, unsure about getting into this sort of discussion on such a long flight.

"The Jews control the media. That's why," said the Frenchman. "Ever since Israel got overrun, the Jews have been hammering at war, war, war. They control the news in America, and the news controls the politicians."

The banker took a deep breath. That was too much fresh meat for a good northeastern liberal to ignore. "That's ridiculous," he said, with an undertone of disdain. "No one controls the media."

"Really? When was the last time you saw al-Zee's viewpoint in your media?" asked the Frenchman.

"Those guys don't have a viewpoint. They just want to kill people. That's just crazy. The media don't put crazy people on TV. It would just make things worse."

"It's very convenient that all two billion of your enemies are crazy. That makes their opinions easy to ignore."

"Look," the banker continued, "you can't put people on TV that are saying, 'If you kill all the Americans and all the Jews you can go to paradise.' That's just common sense. Terrorism isn't a valid opinion."

"How do you know unless you listen to their reasons?"

"Are you in *favor* of terrorism?"

"You are avoiding the question. If the only viewpoints you allowed on television were the ones that you and I agreed with, would that be good?"

"So big deal if the wacko viewpoints don't get on television. You have to do some filtering."

"How many people have to have the same so-called wacko opinions before they are, in your opinion, worthy of media attention?" asked the Frenchman.

"The Muslims aren't *right* just because there are a lot of them."

"We are not discussing the rightness of their ideas, only the newsworthiness."

"Okay, so why do *you* think their views aren't in the media? You're blaming Jews? That's ridiculous. Jews manage maybe five percent of the media, tops. What about the other ninety-five percent? How do you explain why *they* don't run al-Zee's views?"

"Obviously it is more than five percent," said the Frenchman. "There is no other way to explain it. The Jews control the entire media behind the scenes, but they hide it."

"There is a simpler explanation," offered the Avatar as the two businessmen's faces registered an ugly combination of surprise and disdain.

"I'm all ears," said the banker, eager to get the Frenchman off his back.

"Every group controls its own story," explained the Avatar. "Black people control the media's coverage of black issues, Christians control the media's coverage of Christianity, gay people control the media's coverage of gay issues, women control the media's coverage of women's issues, disabled people control the media coverage of disabled people. No reporter would risk his career by crossing any of those groups, or any one of a dozen other organized groups. So when you say that Jews control the media, you don't mean that Jews control the coverage of gay rights, or women's rights, or any other group's story. You simply mean that reporters are human and they know to steer clear of stories that would offend people who could later influence their careers."

The Frenchman and the banker both paused, each hoping the other would jump into the argument. The Avatar seemed surprisingly coherent. After a pause for digestion, the banker looked at the Avatar and asked another question.

"Do you think we should put terrorists' opinions in the media?"

"Yes," replied the Avatar. "The most basic need of any human being is the need to communicate. If you shut down the non-violent channels of communication, people will find alternate channels. Terrorism is communication disguised as warfare. If you treat it as war, you cannot stop it. When you treat it as communication, you have a chance to replace it with something less lethal."

"So you would let some crazy sheikh go on *Crossfire* and explain why all infidels should be killed?"

"I would not only *let* him. I would *require* it. And I would broadcast it often, along with alternative viewpoints. Bad ideas do not survive when they are exposed to the air."

"Let me get this straight," said the banker. "Let's say you have one Muslim and one Jew on television arguing over who should own Jerusalem. The Muslim claims that God gave that land to the Muslims. The Jew says God gave it to the Jews. How the hell does that sort of debate help anything?"

"There is a third view that must be added to the mix whenever the two views are expressed. You must include a scientist who can explain that the notion of 'location' is absurd. Educated people know that in a universe where all the planets are moving and spinning, there is no such thing as a holy 'place' because location is only meaningful as a relationship to fixed objects. In our universe, nothing is fixed. Everything is continually moving. Certainly an omnipotent God would know there could be no such thing as a holy 'place.' Perhaps the dirt and rocks could be holy, some would argue, but if so, then we can find a way to share the dirt. Put it in trucks and drive it to anyone who wants some holy dirt. After all, we are talking about a desert; I am confident there is enough dirt for everyone."

"You're funny, old man," said the banker.

"Everyone is entitled to an opinion," said the Frenchman, not meaning it.

The Frenchman and the banker didn't talk for the rest of the flight.

AVATAR
MEETS AL-ZEE

Qadum looked like any other Middle Eastern city, an undisciplined symphony of traffic, buildings, markets, and people, with a mix of modern steel and local construction materials. But a mile beneath the surface lived a second city, the home of al-Zee. Lower Qadum was built in anticipation of a final battle with the infidels, hardened to withstand a nuclear detonation, self-sustaining, to endure a siege for decades. It was impenetrable by "anyone but God" according to the proud builders.

The Avatar didn't get much of a tour, his head being covered with a hood for the long elevator descent. He could hear the guards talking, and felt their hands gripping his arms from either side. The elevator slowed, and his skin felt heavy as the lift rattled to a stop.

He walked half a mile, maybe more, past the sounds of street activity, down cement hallways where the sound of his footsteps echoed off walls. They passed hydroponic gardens that smelled of vegetables and fertilizer, passed honey merchants and spice vendors. Then he waited, hood removed, in a marble foyer, no one speaking to him directly. Serious-looking people entered and exited through a huge doorway guarded by two of the biggest men he'd ever seen.

A low-level assistant in charge of scheduling approached the marble bench where the Avatar sat, flanked by his handlers. The assistant whispered that al-Zee was available. Guards on either side of the huge door pulled it open in halves. The Avatar and his handlers entered a cavernous room, decorated in a thousand shades of white marble, gold, and shadow. The space dwarfed its most important resident, who sat on an oversize purple cushion, surrounded by five smaller-pillowed advisers competing to see who could look the most menacing.

No one spoke as the handlers guided the Avatar to a pillow in the middle of the group, facing al-Zee. The Avatar sat and studied the face of the world's most dangerous terrorist according to the Christians, and the right hand of God according to two billion Muslims. The Avatar felt his chemistry changing and marveled at the power of al-Zee's charisma. There was something about his eyes, his face, his posture, and his confidence, such that without uttering a word he could alter your body chemistry, make you want to believe him, want to please him. The Avatar was not unaffected, but he recognized it for the illusion that it was.

Al-Zee always let his visitors wait for an uncomfortable period before he started a conversation. He understood the power of his own personality, and he found it useful to let its full impact sink in. But this Avatar fellow seemed odd to al-Zee. He wasn't frightened. It had been years since al-Zee had entertained anyone who didn't fear for his life, and with good reason. He fed his people a continuous stream of rumors about arbitrary executions and torture, partly because doing so made the real thing unnecessary, mostly because it cut down on unnecessary meetings. Al-Zee was a practical man who used violence when he felt God would approve, to better the lives of his people. Toughness was often necessary to preserve order in the Great Caliphate, but when the *appearance* of toughness worked just as well, al-Zee preferred it.

Most people would break under the pressure of al-Zee's silent stare and start babbling. The Avatar just looked and waited for an invitation. Al-Zee was puzzled at first, then competitive, not wanting to be the first to talk. But he also had a full schedule that day. Better to get this over with, he figured, since it was more of a curiosity meeting than a useful one.

"I hear that you know my war plans," he said, in perfect English through a tight-lipped smile. "Is that true?"

"Yes."

"How can you be so sure that you have it right?"

"I wasn't sure until you invited me here," said the Avatar.

Al-Zee laughed. His five advisers were quick to pick up on the cue and laugh too, each one conscious that there could be consequences for laughing overly long or not enough. The laughter was disturbing.

"You know you won't be leaving here alive, don't you?" asked al-Zee, anxious to intimidate his guest.

"I can see why you would feel that way," said the Avatar.

That wasn't the reaction al-Zee wanted. He was looking for some fear, maybe pleading and bargaining. His face turned stern and cold. "Tell me how you found out our war plans."

"I will be happy to tell you. In return, may I ask you one question?"

The advisers shifted and mumbled to each other. No one ever negotiated with al-Zee. It wasn't clear if the Avatar was brave or crazy. Al-Zee stared at the Avatar with a strictness that would feel like punishment to anyone else. Seeing it had no effect, al-Zee smiled. The old man amused him. It had been so long since anyone had spoken to him like a peer that it struck him as funny. "Yes, you may ask me one question later," he said.

"Very good. Thank you," said the Avatar. "Now, about your war plans, you're wondering if someone leaked them to me. The answer is no. I deduced them."

"And how does one deduce so accurately?"

"I assumed that you came to your current position by intelligence and not luck. Then I asked myself what I would do in your position."

"The infidel generals are obviously asking the same questions. Why is it that you figured it out and they haven't?" asked al-Zee.

"They ignored the empty spaces. They focused on what you have done in the past. I looked at what you had *not* done that you *could* have done. For example, you could have used biological weapons in cities on a regular basis. But you knew it would cause such widespread panic in the Christian world that full-blown war would be inevitable, and you wanted to avoid that. You would keep your best weapons for when they would help the most, not as a provocation of war but as a way to stop it if started. You were waiting until you had biological weapons in all the major enemy cities, and you have saved them until there was all-out war, when history would understand why you would unleash them. Your strategy is part public relations and part military, and that is your trademark."

"Well reasoned. Now can you do the same with the infidels' battle plan?"

"First, General Cruz will suppress all media coverage in the Middle East. He'll block all outgoing communication and he'll seal the borders. He wants no pictures of what will happen next. Your armies will try to melt into the civilian population centers, hoping the invaders will be afraid of inflicting civilian casualties. But that won't matter to Cruz, because this is a war of annihilation, not occupation. Once the media are eliminated, Cruz will level city after city. He will destroy sixty percent of the people and one hundred percent of the infrastructure in each city the first day he strikes it. The survivors will live a few months before dying of starvation."

"Your Christian public will never allow the extermination of civilians," al-Zee said confidently.

"That's why the public won't know about it until it's over. Neither will you. There will be no communication or news from any of the cities under attack. They will simply cease to exist."

"Cruz must know where I am by now. Why not attack me directly?"

"He'll send Special Forces to penetrate your defenses and try to kill you at the start of the war. It's a military reflex, standard procedure to cut off the head to kill the snake, as they like to say. But it won't work because you anticipate it. Cruz knows he can't blast you out of your underground fortress. And he knows he can't wait you out. But he can irradiate the city above you, and he can cut off your communications forever. He hopes you will be trapped for decades in your underground shelters, irrelevant to the world. In a way, I think Cruz prefers that ending, knowing you'll be alive but powerless, aware of your complete and utter defeat. Humiliated."

The advisers fidgeted. No one had ever spoken to al-Zee about failure without discovering unpleasant consequences, or so they had heard many times. But al-Zee sat motionless, staring at the Avatar, absorbing this image of the future.

"He will stop his aggression when his own cities begin to die," said al-Zee.

"No, he expects you to attack all the major cities. I told him it would happen. He is already relocating his family members and friends. Cruz sees this as the final battle. Armageddon. He will accept seventy-five percent civilian casualties on his side if he can inflict one hundred percent on your side. He believes the alternative to victory is not peace but waiting for your forces to destroy the Christian economy and infrastructure, until Christian life cannot be supported. He believes God is guiding him, and that victory is justified at any cost."

"You seem sure of yourself," said al-Zee.

"There is one hope to end this," said the Avatar.

"Enlighten me."

"This is a man-made crisis, based on superstition. If minds can be changed, the problem disappears."

"What do you mean by *superstition*?" al-Zee asked with a threatening tone.

"Superstition is a belief in the supernatural, that something exists beyond nature. You and General Cruz believe God is not part of nature, but somehow outside it. That is, by definition, superstition."

"It sounds like an insult," said al-Zee, displeased.

"That's the problem with clarity," responded the Avatar. "It often sounds insulting."

"Why did you volunteer to come here? What did you hope to gain?"

"Time."

"For what?"

"I'm searching for the one who can change opinions. I need a few weeks."

"One person? Who do you believe this one person is?"

"It could be anyone. That's why the search will be difficult."

"One person," al-Zee scoffed. "You have wasted my time. However, I am a man of my word: Ask the question you wanted to ask."

"I was wondering," began the Avatar, pausing until the advisers stopped moving and started listening, "if you had a medical question, whose advice would you seek?"

"*That* is the one thing you want to know?"

"It's a harder question than it seems."

Al-Zee studied the Avatar before answering. Was it a trick question? It didn't matter. "I would see a doctor," he said.

"Thank you," said the Avatar, standing and bowing in respect, signaling his willingness to be led away. The guards entered the circle of advisers, took the Avatar by his arms, and led him toward the exit. When they reached the door, al-Zee ordered, "Don't kill him."

At 3:00 A.M. al-Zee paced the length of his living quarters. His mind visited a thousand places, thinking of the upcoming battle, his strategy, his survival plans, his position in history, and more often than not, the Avatar's question. It bothered him. Normally al-Zee had no trouble sleeping no matter how many people his terror cells had killed that day, no matter how much danger he was in. It was the Avatar's question that got to him. Why would this man who knew so much about his battle plans have only one question, and a trivial one at that? Did he know something about al-Zee's health? Was he a doctor? Was he trying to make some sort of point that completely missed the target? The thought became a clog in al-Zee's mental pipeline. He needed to get it out so he could focus on the more important issues. He hated himself for being obsessed with something so inane.

At 4:00 A.M. al-Zee and three of his guards entered the Avatar's cell and closed the door behind them. The Avatar, seated in a lotus position on the concrete floor, looked up and smiled.

"Explain the question," demanded al-Zee. "What's it mean?"

"I wondered if you seek expert advice before making decisions," said the Avatar.

"Of course I do. Only a fool wouldn't."

"So if you wanted to drill for oil, you might consult a geologist?"

"Get to the point. I need sleep."

"If you wanted to build a structure, you might consult an architect?"

Al-Zee turned bright red, grabbed the Avatar by the shirt, yanked him to his feet, slammed him against the wall, and said, "Tell me what you're after, or you will wish I had already killed you."

The Avatar looked into al-Zee's face with neither fear nor anger. He was pleased to have his full attention. The Avatar smiled. Al-Zee, weary of holding the old man against the wall, and confused by the smile, lowered the Avatar and backed up a step.

"I was just wondering," said the Avatar, "who would you consult if you suspected you were delusional?"

"I'm *not* delusional."

"Can a delusional person always know when he's deluded?"

Al-Zee fumed and snorted. "What is your point?"

"Three billion Christians, Hindus, atheists, and Buddhists think that you *are* deluded about your beliefs. How do you know they're wrong?"

"They *are* wrong. It is *they* who are deluded. They can't see the truth of Allah. But I will change that. They will see the truth in hell."

"Do you think any of them could be taught to see past their delusions while they're still alive?"

"Perhaps. But there are so many."

"So you believe that a person could be taught to recognize his delusion if he is otherwise mentally stable?"

"If he *wants* to see the truth."

"And what kind of expert should such a person seek to help him see past his delusion?"

"A holy scholar."

"Scholars are experts on interpreting history, not identifying delusions in the present. You need an expert in the field of delusion—someone who deals with false perceptions every day. You need a magician."

"*This* is why you came here? To tell me I need a magician?" Al-Zee laughed at the absurdity of it and shook his head.

"No," said the Avatar. "You don't need one, but you will soon find one."

The Avatar sat on the floor and closed his eyes. His body relaxed into instant meditation. Al-Zee looked at him, unsure what to do next. The leader of the Great Caliphate wasn't used to being dismissed. But he saw no reason to continue a discussion that was going nowhere. He opened the door and left, but looked back one more time at the Avatar, who seemed totally at peace. Al-Zee strode past the guard and whispered in Arabic without turning his head, "Kill him."

The guard stood in the doorway looking down at the Avatar, considering the most efficient way to dispatch him without leaving anything to clean. The Avatar, eyes still closed, said, "I'm sorry. Really I am."

"Sorry about what?" the guard asked in broken English.

"It's nothing personal. It's just that I'm on a deadline."

GENERAL CRUZ
PLANS WAR

Cruz's generals busied themselves with the details of war planning: supply lines, target priorities, communications backup, and combat readiness. Cruz had already relocated his family members and the people he cared about from the urban centers that would be targeted by al-Zee. It was done quietly. As far as the neighbors knew, they went on vacation. It set back his plans by three days, just as the Avatar hoped. No matter. War was never meant to be precise.

Cruz's generals used the time to continue running battle simulations, expecting their leader to pick from the most successful ones. The High Commander allowed the generals to believe they were contributing to his decision. It kept them busy and out of his way. The real plan was already decided: extermination. He would reveal his true mission no sooner than necessary. There would be dissent, and some of his generals would have to be replaced immediately. Until then, they were useful, so he pretended to look at the war game simulations and made cosmetic suggestions.

At headquarters, only Waters suspected the truth. He knew Cruz well enough to know when he was interested in something and when he was pretending to be interested. There was no doubt in Waters' mind that none of the plans suggested by Cruz's generals would ever be implemented. And there was even less doubt that Cruz would stop attacking an enemy that had any chance of reconstituting and coming after him again. Cruz liked to do things once. Annihilation was the only battle plan that fit his personality.

Waters had studied military history. He knew that in the past it was practical to strip a defeated army of its biggest weapons and make it harmless. But technology had changed all that. For less than a thousand dollars a terrorist could rig a remote-controlled hobby plane with a GPS guidance system and explosives and send it toward any target within a hundred miles, below radar, virtually unstoppable. The smooth arc of military history had broken. Being the best army no longer meant winning. Cruz was fighting an idea—the idea that killing infidels meant martyrdom and paradise. The idea was like a virus. It couldn't be stopped unless you eliminated all the host bodies. And that, reasoned Waters, had to be Cruz's plan. It wasn't Waters' place to question battle plans, especially ones unspoken. So he did his job, attending to the general's needs.

Cruz sat alone in his office, elbows on the desk, hands supporting his head. It had been a long week. He was incapable of admitting fatigue, but his body was racked with it. He had sat through too many meetings, barked at too many people, made too many decisions, looked at too many casualty estimates. He was burned out. His mind started to drift, opening a doorway for his worst thoughts. In his weakened state he visualized what he was about to do. He imagined mothers and children and the elderly, cats and dogs, people of all sorts, about to be slaughtered or starved to meet his objectives. On some gut level, he actually loved war, especially the thrill of killing people in the heat of combat, but he hated civilian casualties. That lesson was drummed into every soldier—*avoid civilian casualties.* Now he was planning to target civilians, and not just *some* of them but *all* of them. He told himself there was no other way. When he wasn't tired, that line of reasoning worked to calm his emotions. Tonight it emphatically didn't.

Cruz opened his desk cabinet and took out a bottle of whiskey and a glass. It was cheaper than therapy, and faster. He was doing God's work—important work—and there was no way the almighty would begrudge him such a minor vice.

STACEY'S CAFÉ

The Avatar took a hydrocab from the airport to the offices of GIC. Stepping out of the cab, he felt a strange sensation, like a pattern forming, but faint. It seemed to have at least two centers. He had never felt a pattern like this. As the hydrocab pulled away, the Avatar stood on the sidewalk trying to get a lock on the pattern, but he failed. His stomach growled, and the Avatar smiled, realizing that his hunger must have been clogging his intuition. But now the pattern was gone, softening to a vibration. Patterns did that sometimes, rising and falling for no apparent reason. The Avatar walked toward a restaurant next to the GIC building, Stacey's Café. It was the oldest business on the block, looking out of place nestled in the modern architecture of the San Francisco metropolitan area.

The Avatar entered and was greeted by the bartender from behind a large oval bar. "Hi. Can I help you?"

"One for lunch," said the Avatar.

"We're closed between three and five. Can you come back at five?"

A pink-haired woman in her sixties, on the other side of the room, interrupted the Avatar's response. She was waving a half-eaten plate of food at the chef and getting agitated. "Look at this presentation! This is crap! My name is on this business and you want to serve crap! If people want crap they can make it at home!" The chef's eyes were locked in a death stare with the pink-haired woman as she dramatically slapped the dish on the table.

"I want you to care about this place as much as I do! If you don't, I can replace your ass tomorrow!" The pink-haired woman harrumphed and turned away. Then turned back with an after-thought. "That reminds me," she said in a softer voice that seemed as though she was channeling an entirely different person, "have you written down all your recipes so I can fire you any time I want?"

"Almost. I have a few more to do," said the chef.

"Very good. Give me a hug."

The pink-haired lady hugged the chef, who smiled and chuckled before returning to the kitchen. "I have new pictures of my baby if you want to see them," said the chef over his shoulder.

"Nah. But if you get some pictures of your cat, bring them in. I love cats. Kids, not so much." The chef laughed again as he disappeared into the kitchen.

The Avatar watched the scene in its entirety before looking at the bartender and saying, "I didn't realize you were closed. I will find something from a vending machine."

The pink-haired woman moved in on him. "Vending machine? You walk into my restaurant and say you want to eat from a frickin' vending machine? What is your story, blanket-boy?" The Avatar just looked at her and smiled. She said, "I'm Stacey. I own this joint. Well, technically I have a partner, but he

isn't worth a damn. Sit down and we'll make you something."
Stacey gestured toward a table in the empty dining room. The
Avatar complied, taking a seat in the middle of a sea of white
tablecloths. Stacey opened the menu in front of him and started
pointing. "You'll have one of these. No, forget that, I just tore the
chef a new one about this dish, so take this one. That's my
favorite."

"I should eat *your* favorite food?" asked the Avatar, enjoying
the show.

"*Everyone* should eat my favorite food, Gandhi, unless you're
on a hunger strike. You aren't on a hunger strike, are you?"

"I don't go to restaurants for my hunger strikes," the Avatar
answered.

"*One vegetable croûte!*" yelled Stacey in the general direction of
the kitchen. A frightened line cook nodded.

"And a glass of water, please," said the Avatar.

"You'll have wine."

"I only want water."

"One Chardonnay."

Stacey made hand signals to the bartender, who was still wip-
ing water spots off the bar glasses. He nodded and started to pour
a Chardonnay. Stacey pulled out a chair and sat down across from
the Avatar. "I think I have a headache or a tumor or something. I
gained two pounds this week and my hair is falling out in
clumps. And I have gas. Don't say I didn't warn you."

"Thank you for the warning."

"I don't know how I do this job every day. I'm going to quit.
I swear I am. Except it wouldn't work because I own the place.

I'd fire my ass if I could, but I don't want to pay the unemployment benefits to myself."

An attractive twenty-something server, off duty, approached the table carrying her apron. The Avatar noticed that her makeup was an unusual choice, and it was the second time he had seen that distinctive makeup choice that day. Her shoes looked familiar too, and her hair had the pink tint that was in style lately. He detected the first signs of a pattern, but it was interrupted.

"Iron your shirt, you slob," lectured Stacey.

"I just ironed it," protested the server.

"No, Stevie Wonder ironed that shirt."

"Who's Stevie Wonder?" asked the server.

"Ai-yi-yi. You know nothing. Iron your shirt again."

Stacey dismissed the server with a wave of her hand and turned to the Avatar. "So, are you a nut or what? I need to hear a good story. My television has been broken for a week. My pet chicken chewed through the cables."

"I'm an Avatar."

"And that would be ... what, like a captain?"

"Something like that."

"Okay, Captain. Hey, I like that. Your name is Captain now."

The line cook delivered the Avatar's dish to the table. Stacey's eyes locked on to the dish, and she took a deep breath. "Are those mashed potatoes? I told you to use Yukon potatoes! Did your mother drop you on your head when you were little or do you just choose to ignore me?"

The Avatar smiled at the cook, who mouthed a silent "ouch" and scurried away.

"So what's your story? Tell me everything. I'll know if you're lying."

"Do you really want to know?" the Avatar asked before putting a bite of asparagus in his mouth.

"I wouldn't say it if I didn't want to know. I've seen a billion people walk through these doors and I can tell when someone has a story. It's all over your face. Cough it up."

"A war is about to break out."

"That terrorist thing? They bomb us, we bomb them. Tell me something I don't know."

"You don't know that two billion people will die if the war happens. I plan to stop it."

"Oookay, sorry I asked." Stacey sat back in her chair and watched the Avatar chew.

"Delicious," he said.

"Of course." Stacey continued to stare at the Avatar, and he allowed it, not showing the least bit of discomfort. A minute passed and she couldn't take it anymore. "You're scaring me, Captain."

"What took you so long?"

"You weren't lying, were you?"

The Avatar nodded. She was as good at reading faces as she claimed.

"How can a guy like *you* stop a war? You couldn't even feed yourself until I decided to have pity on your ass. And you dress like a hobo on crack. What's up with that?"

"Would it be okay if I answered the first question?"

Stacey laughed. "Okay. If you do a good job on that I'll let the other ones slide. Go."

"Think of humanity as a giant software program. Our bodies are the hardware and our ideas are the software. Sometimes our software gets a virus."

"What the hell are you talking about, Captain?"

"Religious misinterpretations. People who are infected with flawed religious ideas can infect others, especially their children. The religions spread and mutate, until there are thousands of different religious ideas, most of them harmless, some healthy and helpful, but others quite deadly. When the deadly ones reach a critical mass, they threaten the whole."

"The hole?"

"The entirety."

"Good, because I hate holes. So what do you do about this virus?"

"I'm looking for the reboot button, metaphorically speaking. I'm looking for the one person who is connected to everyone else in a chain of influence. The Prime Influencer. That is why I am visiting GIC today. Their computers are doing a search for that person now."

"So you're saving the world?" Stacey asked.

"That's the plan."

"Okay, so suppose you find this Prime Influencer person. What are you going to do, change his opinion somehow? I don't think so. I've been around a long time and I've never seen anyone change his opinion just because some rag-wearing nut tells him to."

"You don't believe people can change their opinions?" asked the Avatar.

"Come on. Who buys books written by conservatives? Conservatives. Who buys books written by liberals? Liberals. People only listen to what they want to hear. No one changes anyone's mind."

"Even if the argument is very good?"

"Hasn't happened. Never will."

The Avatar sat back in his chair, adjusting his napkin on his lap. "I can see why you would have that view. But in reality, everyone knows *one* person who can change his opinion on a particular topic—usually a different person for each topic. It is not the argument or the logic that matters to people, but the source. Humans are driven by examples, by role models, not by logic."

"So you're saying someone could make me a devil worshipper even if I didn't want to be? That's nutty."

"A year ago you would have said that no one could convince you to wear pink-tinted hair. But you seem to have embraced that trend enthusiastically."

"Hey, Captain, don't be knocking my hair. And besides, I wasn't copying anyone. I just like the color."

"Okay."

"Why don't you talk to the religious people and find out why they believe nonsense? Whatever magic they're using to brain-wash each other must be working," said Stacey.

"You don't believe in God?" asked the Avatar.

"Not one that matters."

"How could God not matter?"

"Let's say there's some powerful big ol' God that created everything. He must be a moron because somehow he gave everyone a different idea of what he wants. I mean if you're omnipotent, the least you could do is tell us which holy book to read. He can't even get the little crap right."

The Avatar decided to test her line of thinking with an argument that was common albeit flawed. "If God exists he must be smart to design the world so perfectly. Everything is in perfect balance. If any of our natural laws were altered in the least, life would be unsustainable. Only an omnipotent genius could create such perfect balance in the laws of physics."

"Physics shmysics. If God is so smart, why do you fart?"

The Avatar waited for the rest of the argument, but there was none. The two strangers stared at each other for a moment before being overcome with a wave of laughter that brought both of them to tears. The restaurant staff all stopped and watched as the unlikely duo convulsed. After minutes of uncontrolled laughing, the kind that clears the mind and makes your feet warm, the Avatar smiled and took out his universal payment card.

"Save your money, Captain. You're going to need it for the hospital bills if you keep insulting people's hair. This one's on me."

As the Avatar walked toward the exit, the bartender smiled and said, "Thanks for coming, Captain."

MACKEY'S PROGRESS

Eric Mackey met the Avatar in the lobby of GIC and told the guard to issue a security badge. He was obviously agitated. Mumbling turned into loud anger on the elevator ride up. "It can't be done. Too many variables. I've tried a dozen approaches. I can't find a way to isolate the lines of influence in the database. There just isn't enough data. Every time I think I'm close, bam, something blows up."

"You will find it," assured the Avatar.

"I'd better find it fast, because it's getting pretty obvious to everyone that I'm not working on my job. But more to the point, it's *not possible.*"

"It *is* possible. I can feel it."

"What do you mean you can 'feel it'? Are you a programmer? You dress like one."

"No. But I have a distinct feeling that the answer is here. I can sense the pattern as I approach the building."

"Good Lord, you're a lunatic and I'm working for you. What's that make me?"

"Why are you helping me?"

"Because I feel like it's my personal responsibility to save the world from idiots. I don't know how these morons can believe in God anyway. The whole war would be unnecessary if they just woke up and smelled the science. Evolution has been proven a hundred times over. You'd think that would be proof enough."

"Evolution has been proven?" the Avatar asked as they walked down the corridor of cubicles.

"Don't start with me."

"How do you define evolution in scientific terms?" asked the Avatar.

"It's the gradual change of species over time. That's the quick and dirty definition."

"How do you define 'time' in scientific terms?" asked the Avatar.

"You know what time is."

"According to physicists, time is an artifact of our percep- tions, not an objective quality of the universe. So evolution, according to you, is defined as the gradual change of species over *something that doesn't exist*."

"Clever. I have to think about that. You're freaky, dude."

"I have one more question."

"Shoot."

"If you believe in evolution, then you believe that some part of the human population will eventually evolve to a new species, don't you?" asked the Avatar.

"Well, I guess so. Probably more than one species."

"Do you see the beginnings of that evolution yet? Have you spotted any people who are on their way to being a new species?"

"Hmm . . . not really. Maybe some people are getting taller or something, but no one is growing wings. But if you're saying that evolution is false because you can't see it happening, that's a bogus argument. We wouldn't necessarily notice any small changes in our lifetimes."

"Actually, you wouldn't notice any large changes either, apparently."

"Like what?"

"Humans have already split into two distinct groups that could, according to your understanding of time, become separate species."

"Who are these groups?"

"I call one group Awares and the other Gullibles. The Gullibles believe anything that makes them feel good, no matter how unproven or irrational. Awares are the opposite, persuaded only by reason and evidence. Awares will sometimes believe things that are unproven, for practical reasons, but never because it makes them feel good. The two groups overlap now. Most people have a combination of both. But the people at the extremes, the true Awares and true Gullibles, will increasingly mate only with their own kind. The Awares will consider the Gullibles too backward for mating. The Gullibles will consider the Awares too godless and immoral. In a million years the Awares will be a separate branch of humanity fighting for survival."

"Why would the Awares have to fight to survive? They sound like the smart ones."

"Awares are a small group already, and they tend to breed slowly compared to Gullibles. Their survival depends on the majority allowing them to survive. And sooner or later the Gullibles will feel threatened by the Awares."

"Okay, but I'm not worrying about that now. I just wanted to tell you that I don't think there's enough data to find the one you're looking for. If it was possible, I could do it. But it isn't."

"The answer is here," said the Avatar.

"Why should I believe you? I don't even know your last name."

"You've listened to my story, and like a good skeptic, you judged it highly unlikely to be true because it sounds so extraordinary. But if I'm right, and two billion lives are at stake, you know you couldn't live with yourself if you didn't at least try. And besides, you can't resist the challenge. You can practically smell the solution, and it's eating at you that you can't nail it."

"Screw you."

"I will be back for your answer in two days."

HOW ISRAEL FELL

Al-Zee enjoyed the daylight of Qadum, knowing it could be his last chance to feel the sun. His bodyguards cut a wide swath through the outdoor marketplace, staring down anyone who dared to look directly at their leader. Al-Zee made a point to stop at every other merchant's stand and examine the goods. The bodyguards purchased merchandise on his behalf, as a show of respect. It was good public relations. His mood was somber, weighed down by thoughts of the upcoming war. He replayed in his mind the path of his life and wondered what he could have done differently.

Al-Zee was educated in a madrassa, where he learned to be a believer. He was an exceptional student who had memorized every line of the Koran by the time he was eight years old. When he was a teen he was already active in the underground efforts to destroy Israel and overthrow the pro-Western dictators of the Arab countries. By the age of nineteen he had become a protégé of the most successful planner in Al Qaeda and soon found himself running operations of his own with spectacular success. He wanted to become a martyr, but his partners in Jihad recognized him as too valuable to waste.

His most notable early success was the simultaneous assassination of President Kendal of the United States and Prime Minister Kent of the United Kingdom in 2010. It took three years of planning to place the tons of explosives under city blocks in both Washington, D.C., and London. And it took another year to create fake political fund-raising events that would lure his targets to the traps at precisely the same times.

After American Special Forces, operating on a tip, located and killed the leader of Al Qaeda, al-Zee was the logical successor— young, brilliant, completely dedicated to the cause. He immediately put into place the "Israel Strategy," which was to become his springboard to complete control of the Middle East.

The Israel Strategy involved convincing the Palestinians to accept a disingenuous peace in return for international promises of massive reconstruction aid. They would wait, letting prosperity accomplish what terrorist attacks could not. Al-Zee was the first Muslim leader to realize that the only way they could lose the fight with Israel was to continue fighting. Peace meant inevitable victory; it just required patience. Al-Zee's reputation allowed him to preach patience to an impatient people. His credibility was unapproachable. So they made peace, and they waited.

Demographics favored the Muslims, who were having children at three times the rate of the Jewish population, thanks to financial inducements arranged by al-Zee. By 2035, it was clear that Muslims were heading toward a voting majority in Israel. The Israeli government hoped to solve the problem by restricting voting rights for non-Jews. This was exactly what al-Zee had foreseen. Israel was filled with, and surrounded by, a massive population of angry young men who preferred death to the apartheid and humiliation they were being asked to accept. After years of lying low, al-Zee focused the anger of the majority, who were by then universally armed, and working and living amongst the Jewish minority.

The overrun lasted less than two days. It was mostly hand-to-hand fighting with knives, small arms, and homemade explosives. The military was helpless because the violence was everywhere at the same time, in every block, every street, every housing development. Human waves of martyrs stormed military bases. Over a million Muslims died that day, eventually exhausting the ammunition of the Israeli army and the armed Jewish civilians. With their superior numbers, the element of surprise, and a willingness to die as martyrs, al-Zee's citizen Jihadists prevailed. The Jewish Israeli men stayed and fought to the last, along with most of the fighting age women. The older women and children were allowed to escape on foot, streaming out of the cities and towns and eventually ending up in refugee camps.

To the rest of the world it became known as the Second Holocaust, an unfathomable and black moment in history, dwarfing the First Holocaust in both scope and savagery. It happened so quickly that the world didn't know how to respond. By the end of the second day there were so few Jews left in Israel that military intervention seemed useless. Countries condemned the atrocities in the strongest words, but they were only words. Some countries threatened embargoes but needed the oil and so found reasons to back off. A feeling of shame and helplessness gripped the Judeo-Christian world, plunging it into a collective mental depression, and making it ripe for the rise of a man like General Horatio Cruz.

Al-Zee's status as the architect of the victory over Israel grew to enormous heights. He turned his influence against the pro-Western governments of the Arab countries. The "corrupt leaders," as he called them, were soon deposed and replaced by al-Zee's people. Al-Zee believed that his success was proof that Allah was on his side. He found it harder and harder to distinguish between his own opinions and those that were coming directly from Allah.

Now the endgame was approaching. Peace with the Christian Alliance was impossible because his own citizens would kill him if he even suggested peace. The Muslims felt like winners, and they couldn't imagine that God would let them lose after letting them win for so long. Al-Zee couldn't win a conventional war against Cruz's military superiority, but he knew he would survive underground while the world above him was annihilated. That was his plan, should the war become unstoppable. Two billion of his followers would perish aboveground. But in the end, in a few decades, after all civilization aboveground was killed, starved, or died of disease, only Muslims from belowground would be left to repopulate the world as Allah intended. It would be the dawn of the Final Age, when Islam would rule the world for the rest of time.

The sounds and colors of the marketplace began to melt together for al-Zee as he walked, captured by his own thoughts. His arms and legs were heavy with fatigue, and his breathing was shallow, but he tried not to show it. He even managed a smile now and then. He walked past merchants hawking vegetables, clothing, guns, and herbs. There were street performers too, ever since al-Zee had passed a law allowing more forms of entertainment. He stood and watched a juggler manipulate a ball, a clay pot, and a flaming torch. His bodyguards dropped some coins in the entertainer's bowl.

And then al-Zee saw him. A chill ran the length of his spine, an odd sensation in hundred-degree heat. His bodyguards noticed al-Zee's sudden distress and looked around to see if there was a threat. Noticing nothing unusual, they turned to examine more closely where al-Zee was looking, at a street magician.

The magician recognized al-Zee by his distinctive clothing and the cluster of bodyguards, and bowed respectfully before offering a show. "Would you like to see this camel disappear?" he asked, motioning to a raggedy-looking beast behind him. The bodyguards laughed. They knew a camel couldn't disappear, but they appreciated the magician's sense of humor and anticipated the punch line.

Al-Zee said nothing. He just stared at the magician, trying to remember exactly what the Avatar had said. Al-Zee figured it was a coincidence that he'd noticed this magician today, nothing more. There was probably a magician on every street corner, although he had never noticed one in Qadum.

"I'll take that as a yes," said the magician as he guided the camel to his side and started his act. "This simple camel of flesh and blood and bone," he began, until a worried-looking messenger on foot interrupted the show.

"I have an important message for al-Zee," exhaled the messenger toward a bodyguard before gulping more oxygen. "The old man, the one named Avatar, has escaped."

"*Escaped?*" asked al-Zee.

"Yes," said the messenger, heart beating and eye twitching. "Both guards are dead. We found them today. It looks like they shot each other. We think it happened yesterday or the day before. No one knows."

Al-Zee looked at the ground, trying to process the news. The Avatar must have had help. There was no other explanation.

"We must return now," he said to his bodyguards before taking a step and stopping. "Wait." Al-Zee turned to the magician, only to see him standing alone, the camel already gone. "Where is the camel?"

"It disappeared," said the magician with undisguised pride.

"To where?" al-Zee asked, impatiently.

"I . . . um . . . am not at liberty to tell you. It's against the magicians' code."

Al-Zee glared at the magician. He didn't need to repeat the question. His look was enough. The magician's knees started to shake, and he felt asthmatic. As much as he didn't want to violate the magicians' code, he also wanted to live. He hoped there was a middle ground. Maybe al-Zee would be satisfied with seeing the camel return.

"You will see him again soon," the magician stuttered. "When you least expect it." Indeed, that was how the illusion was designed. The magician would normally make a few more things disappear: a hat, an olive branch, and a colorful scarf. When the camel returned, it would be wearing the scarf and hat, with the olive branch in its teeth. The whole act would be ruined if he brought back the camel now, already adorned with items that hadn't yet disappeared.

Several thoughts flooded al-Zee's mind. He wanted to punish the magician, but it would be bad for his image, and he would regret it later. Al-Zee decided that it didn't matter. It was just a magic trick, and he didn't want the Avatar or the magician to get in his head. He had more important things to do. Al-Zee grumbled and turned to leave. The magician's words stuck in his mind. *You will see him again soon.*

Not likely, thought al-Zee, exiting the market.

Al-Zee's anger subsided as he passed through the extensive security layers to Lower Qadum. By the time he reached his living quarters he was almost calm. He didn't like mysteries, especially on the precipice of war. Why had the Avatar risked his life to ask a trivial question? How had he escaped? How did the Avatar know that al-Zee would meet a magician, given that al-Zee's walk in the city hadn't been planned?

Al-Zee, alone in his private quarters, arranged a prayer mat on the floor and prepared to kneel. He looked forward to being alone, a rarity lately. A hard sound interrupted him, echoing off the marble walls from a source unknown. Perhaps a bodyguard was resting his gun against the door. Al-Zee knelt, then succumbed to the temptation to investigate. He opened his door to see the bodyguards standing twenty feet away, guns over their shoulders. They assured him that no one had been near the door. Al-Zee closed the door and considered that maybe something in the washroom had fallen over, or perhaps the ventilation system was expanding from the heat; sometimes it did that. Strange sounds weren't the only intrusion. Now he could smell something. Something familiar—an odor he recognized from childhood. Wet camel hair.

Al-Zee walked cautiously toward his washroom, not sure if he could still smell the wet camel hair or not. It felt as much a memory as a smell. He heard another noise similar to the first, this time clearly from the interior of his quarters. There was only one place from which both the sound and the smell could be originating—inside his washroom. Suddenly al-Zee recognized the noises. They were hooves on stone, like a camel shifting its weight. The magician's words floated back into al-Zee's mind. *You will see him again soon.* Apparently this was part of the trick. Obviously the bodyguards were in on it, mistakenly thinking that al-Zee would appreciate the humor of a camel appearing in his washroom. He was not amused. There would be consequences.

The hallway to the washroom was dark. Al-Zee approached cautiously, angrily. He could see shapes through the open washroom door. Darkness took form, morphing in his mind until the shapes had substance and purpose. There it was: the silhouette of a camel's neck, head, and ears, mostly obscured by dark.

Al-Zee turned and stormed to the main door, yanked it open, and lit into his bodyguards. They had no idea what he was yelling about, but it soon became clear that he wanted something removed from his washroom and he wasn't amused. They ran in that direction, hoping to figure it out on the way. They had never seen their leader so angry, and they had seen all of his moods. Incandescent lights flooded the washroom and illuminated the corners. The bodyguards looked around, then exchanged nervous glances. Someone would have to tell al-Zee that there was nothing unusual in his washroom. No one wanted that job.

MENSA

General Cruz told Waters to enter his office and close the door behind him. Cruz opened a cabinet and took out a bottle of whiskey and two glasses.

"Sit down, Lieutenant," he ordered in a softer voice than normal.

Waters pulled out a chair and sat. Cruz placed a glass of whiskey in front of him, then settled in the big chair behind the desk before downing a mouthful.

"Drink it," Cruz ordered.

"I don't drink, sir," answered Waters.

"Why not? Do you have alcoholics in your family?" asked Cruz.

"Not anymore, sir," said Waters, looking away.

"Right. Sorry." Cruz took another drink and plunked the glass on the desk, leaned forward on his elbows, and looked into Waters' eyes. "Tell me what you think of this whole thing, Lieutenant."

"What whole thing, sir?"

"You know what I mean, damn it. The war. Tell me what you think of the war."

"I'm just one opinion, sir."

"You're also the only person who isn't afraid of me. Hell, you're not afraid of anything. You're dead inside, Waters. And that makes you useful to me. You're the only one who won't lie."

"I doubt that is true, sir."

"See that? You're the only person to tell me I'm wrong in five years, except for that old fool with the blanket. By the way, where is he?"

"We followed him to one of al-Zee's sleeper cells. That's how we confirmed that al-Zee has biological weapons. The whole basement was full of the stuff, and enough GPS-guided microplanes to spread them over the entire city."

"Where's the old coot now?"

"We lost him in Qadum. We think he went to see al-Zee."

"He won't be coming back from that visit," Cruz observed before taking another hit of whiskey. "So tell me what you think of the war, Waters."

"Your battle planning is very thorough," said Waters.

"You know that's not what I mean," said Cruz, his voice trailing off, staring at his glass and rotating it with one hand.

Waters hesitated, letting his thoughts form, not quite sure what would come out of his mouth until he heard it himself. Cruz was the most powerful man in the history of civilization. He was tired, clearly uncertain, starting to get tipsy, and for the first time since Waters had known him, he was unpredictable.

"Are you asking me if the war is *right*?" asked Waters.

"Don't make me say it."

Waters took a deep breath and stood up, pacing, choosing his words carefully before releasing them.

"You believe God is on your side," said Waters.

"I do."

"Why?"

"Because I'm fighting evil."

"Doesn't al-Zee feel exactly the same way?"

"Waters, are you going to tell me God is on the side of the terrorists?"

Waters paced and looked at the wall art, the floor, everywhere but directly at Cruz, who was refilling his glass.

"What if you're *both* wrong?"

"We can't *both* be fighting evil if we're fighting each other."

"I don't think that's necessarily true, but it's not what I mean. I mean, what if God doesn't exist?"

Cruz laughed a little too loudly and took another drink. "Any idiot knows God exists, Waters. That part is obvious."

"Perhaps. But there's something that has always bothered me."

"Let's not get philosophical, Lieutenant. We don't need to know how many angels can dance on the head of a pin."

"You said any idiot knows that God exists, and I think you're right. But here's what bothers me . . ."

Waters spun the computer monitor around to face his side of the desk and pulled the keyboard closer. With a few keystrokes he called up the home page for the local branch of Mensa, the social organization of people with genius IQs. With a few clicks he sent Mensa's phone number to the desk phone and pushed the speaker button. Cruz had one of the few unrestricted phones in the world. Unlike the civilian population, he could call anyone. The call rang through to Mensa. Cruz just watched.

"Hello, this is Mensa," said a female voice.

"This is Lieutenant Ben Waters. Would you mind if I asked you a question?"

"No problem. We get that a lot."

"Do you believe God exists?"

"Nope. Next question."

Cruz didn't like where this was going. "Are you *in* Mensa or just the operator?" he asked.

"We're all here for the weekly meeting. I was closest to the phone."

"What about the other people in your organization? Do *they* believe in God?"

"Hold on, I'll ask them."

Cruz and Waters waited, not looking at each other. Half a minute passed before the voice returned.

"Depends how you define God."

Cruz jumped in. "We're talking about the God of creation, intelligent, all-powerful, listens to prayers, heaven and hell."

"Okay, I'll try that. Hold on."

Cruz and Waters waited another minute.

"No takers," said the voice.

"What do you mean 'no takers'?" asked Cruz defensively.

"No one here believes in that kind of God," said the voice.

"How many people are there?" asked Waters.

"Twenty-three. Why are you asking?" asked the Mensan.

Waters responded, "I read in *Newsweek* that smart people are less likely to believe in God. There was some sort of study."

"Oh, yeah. That's true," said the Mensan. "But it's not *because* of intelligence. It's because smart people have more exposure to science. People who have exposure to scientific training usually become nonreligious, unless they have some vested interest. I mean, the Pope is a pretty bright guy, but no matter how much he studies science, he's not going to become an atheist."

"What about faith?" Cruz asked. "Don't any of you brainiacs have faith?"

"Have you ever looked up the definition of 'faith' in the dictionary?"

"I know what faith is," said Cruz.

"I don't think you do. The dictionary definition of faith involves believing in something *without evidence*. You and I have never met, but I'll bet every penny to my name that you believe in God *because* of evidence, not *without* it. For example, I'll bet you see the Bible as evidence that God exists. You've probably perceived some link between your prayers and your successes, and that seems to be more evidence of God. Maybe you think that because the world seems so well designed, that's evidence of an intelligent creator. If you're influenced by evidence, it's not faith."

"If it's not faith, what is it?" asked Waters.

"It's a really, really, really bad way to do science." The Mensan laughed. "You might not need the scientific method to decide what shirt to wear, but when you're talking about life and death and the hereafter, you ought to be putting a little more rigor into evaluating the evidence."

"Evidence exists, and I can't ignore it, but I would believe in God without any. I do have faith," said Cruz.

"We have a rule in the local group that we don't call anyone stupid. But if you look up the definition of 'stupid' in the dictionary, it will say 'unreasoned thinking.' That includes believing in something without evidence."

"I thought you weren't allowed to call me stupid," said Cruz.

"You're the one who said you have faith. The dictionary called you stupid. I'm just connecting the dots."

Waters thanked the Mensan and ended the call. He and Cruz both leaned back in their chairs. Cruz didn't know exactly what to say.

"And *that's* what bothers me," said Waters.

GIC BOMBING

When al-Zee's guards looked for the camel in his washroom, they found no trace that one had ever been there. Al-Zee was so angry he thought his forehead would burst. He'd distinctly seen the camel's head in the darkness, but he couldn't deny that it was no longer there. This was no time to be losing his mind. He needed answers, and he needed them before the war started.

"Find the Avatar," he yelled at his chief of security. "Put the word out on the network."

Despite the best efforts of his enemies, al-Zee maintained full communications with his terror groups via the Internet. Cruz's intelligence forces electronically searched every message that crossed the Internet, but their sniffing programs were looking for text, keywords, key phrases, and encrypted files. Al-Zee's people thwarted the filters by simply handwriting their messages on photographs of landscapes, scanning in the entire pictures, and sending them as e-mail attachments. A human could easily read the handwritten message on the photo, but a computer wouldn't find enough regularity or structure to identify where a tree ended and a letter began.

Only one response to the Avatar query came back, from a hydrocab driver pseudo-named Hector Rodriguez. He didn't know where the Avatar was, but he knew he was doing business at GIC.

"Destroy it," ordered al-Zee. "And he'll find us."

Although GIC was the data collection center for identifying terrorists, the building was virtually unprotected save for a security guard in the lobby. The data was safely housed in fortified underground bunkers in another state, with full backups in a third state. The thing that kept GIC safe from terror attacks was that the citizens of the Christian Alliance hated it more than the terrorists feared it. Citizens didn't like the fact that the government had access to all of their transactions and preferences. It was an ugly violation of privacy. That had been a good enough reason for al-Zee to avoid targeting it in the past. Anything that turned the citizens of the Christian Alliance against their own government was good for him. But now he had a higher priority. He wanted to find the Avatar.

The drone flew close to the ground, avoiding radar and the automated particle beam defense grid. Terror drones were always painted black and designed to make a frightening screech as they passed overhead. Terror was the objective, and if you could generate extra terror on the way to the target, all the better from al-Zee's perspective. Hydrocabs pulled into alleys and side streets for protection as the drone screamed overhead. Its guidance system was so accurate, and its internal radar so precise, that it zigzagged around buildings and deftly avoided street poles before turning abruptly and heading directly for the main lobby entrance of GIC headquarters. The small nose cone explosive detonated on impact with the door, creating a hole for its payload to enter before doing its work.

The science of GPS-guided bombing had become sophisti-cated. The amount of explosives was carefully adjusted to gut the target building and blow out the windows without much damage to adjacent buildings. Al-Zee always operated with precision because doing so sent a message of competence. He wanted people to know he could destroy anything he wanted, anytime he wanted, without damaging anything nearby.

At 2:30 P.M. Eric Mackey looked up from his club sandwich at Stacey's Café just in time to see his place of employment disinte-grate. The shock wave blew out windows and sent the patrons to the floor. A thick cloud of construction debris filled the restaurant as the customers and employees staggered for the exit, holding napkins and aprons over their mouths, coughing, crying, and screaming.

Mackey picked up his laptop computer from the floor and followed the crowd to the exit. He knew that everyone in the GIC building was dead. He knew grief would hit him in a few minutes, but right now he was in survival mode. He jogged half a block to get away from the worst of the dust.

"Now it's personal," he muttered to himself.

A pink-haired woman staggered out of the cloud of debris, coughing and knocking the crud off her shoulders and hair. Her phone was already at her ear, and she was cursing at her insurance agent.

"Well of course you haven't heard about it because it just happened. I want an adjuster down here in fifteen minutes. I've been paying you jokers for thirty years and now it's your turn. I want to reopen tomorrow. . . . Okay, Wednesday at the latest. . . . Call me when you have the check."

Mackey stood and stared at the remains of his building, clutching his laptop. Stacey clipped her phone to her wrist and stood next to him, still knocking debris off her sweater.

"About your lunch. It's on me today."

"Thanks," said Mackey reflexively, not really registering the absurdity.

"I thought you said they'd never bomb your building."

"I don't understand. Everyone knows the data isn't in the building. And the public hates us more than the terrorists do. It doesn't make sense. Al-Zee always picks his targets by PR."

"He's after someone," said Stacey. "Maybe it's you."

"I don't think so. If they wanted me they would have made sure I was in the building."

"Well, aren't we full of ourselves. I was just kidding. Why would al-Zee care about you?"

"I built the data-mining algorithms. I know more about the system than anyone on Earth. But they're not after me. They aren't that sloppy."

"Then why'd they do it? You're so smart with your algorithms. Sound it out."

Mackey shifted his weight from one foot to the other and thought about it. Al-Zee's attacks were always messages. They were never random. He was trying to tell someone something.

The rubble scanners were already in place, creating three-dimensional models of the debris and directing rescuers with laser pointers. Only two minutes had passed, and already most of the rescue equipment and crews were on the scene working. Bombings had become so common that cleanup was a profitable business. There was a cleanup company in every corner of the city, equipped to handle freshly demolished buildings. Men in HAZMAT suits dragged multipurpose devices that could quickly dig, lift, cut, or move concrete and steel. Each time the rubble scanner put another laser dot on the pile, a team closed in on it and started tunneling with macabre efficiency. The sirens had already stopped because everyone who needed to be there was, including the mobile hospital trucks.

"It's a message," mumbled Mackey.

"What?" asked Stacey while looking at her damaged restaurant.

"A message. Al-Zee is trying to tell someone something."

"And he doesn't have e-mail?" asked Stacey.

"It's a message to someone who can't be reached any other way. Someone who has a connection to this building but wouldn't be in it now."

"You're right," said the Avatar, now standing behind Mackey.

Mackey turned to the Avatar, surprised to see him, and not trusting the thoughts that were connecting in his brain.

"It's you?" Mackey asked.

"We'll know in a minute," said the Avatar, scanning the street behind him, fixing his gaze on a hydrocab that crept up to them, driven by Hector Rodriguez, the only remaining member of al-Zee's local cell that hadn't been captured or killed by Cruz's forces. Stacey, on her phone again, wandered off to tell the bread deliveryman he could skip today. Hector pressed a button on his steering wheel, and the passenger door swung open.

"I'm being invited to a meeting. Come with me to the airport," the Avatar said to Mackey.

Hector heard the invitation and gestured emphatically that the Avatar was to travel alone. The Avatar acknowledged Hector's distress and turned to explain. "This is Eric Mackey. He knows you work for al-Zee. He can read your hydrocab ID plate. Do you want to leave him here?"

Hector cursed in Arabic and waved a thumb toward the backseat as if to say, Get in.

"Seriously?" Mackey asked the Avatar.

"Ride with me to the airport. We need to talk."

"If he's al-Zee's guy, won't he kill us?"

"His job is to take me to al-Zee."

"Okay, let me rephrase that. Won't he kill *me*?"

"He intends to. Either now or later."

The Avatar gestured toward Hector, who was pointing a large handgun at Mackey.

"Remind me to thank you for getting me into this," Mackey said as he bundled into the hydrocab.

The Avatar joined Mackey in the backseat and closed the door. Hector tucked the gun under his seat and started to drive.

"Are you trying to get me killed?" asked Mackey.

"Actually, I saved you. His gun has a silencer. The streets are littered with wounded and dead already. He would have killed you back there, and no one would have noticed, if I hadn't insisted that you come with me."

"So, what, now he just whacks me after he drops you off?" asked Mackey, agitated.

"No. He will realize that you're working with me. And he'll reason that if al-Zee wants me alive, which he obviously does for now, he might need you alive too if we're working on the same task. He's trained not to ask what al-Zee or any other part of the organization is planning, in case one of them gets caught and interrogated. So he can't ask us what your role in this is. In the face of uncertainty, he will be unusually receptive to the opinion of anyone who is certain."

Mackey could see Hector's eyes in the rearview mirror. He was livid, squeezing the steering wheel so hard that his fingers looked deformed.

"And this certain person is you?" asked Mackey, not convinced that this theory would hold.

"Yes," said the Avatar to Mackey, then leaned forward to talk directly to Hector. "After you drop me off, take Mackey anywhere he wants to go. Your leader needs me and I need him."

Hector's shoulders slumped, and he squeezed out a sigh of resignation.

"Now, on to more important things," said the Avatar to Mackey.

"Right. More important than my life," said Mackey, rolling his eyes.

"I assume you can continue your work despite the bombing."

"The computers are fine. But it's hopeless. There's no algorithm that can find this one 'influencer' person you're looking for. There just isn't enough data to make all the connections."

"There must be," said the Avatar, showing frustration for the first time. "I could feel the pattern when I approached your building."

"Okay, that's all very spooky, and I have no idea what you're talking about."

"I just mean that I am confident you can do it."

"Well, I appreciate that. But confidence doesn't write code. I'm telling you it can't be done."

"Are you telling Hector that I have no further use for you?" asked the Avatar.

"Uh, no. I'll take another look at it. Maybe I overlooked something. Never happened before, but maybe this time."

As they spoke, all of the GIC victims' bodies were recovered from the site, the debris entirely removed, and new construction crews were in place, all in less than an hour. The Christian Alliance spared no expense to fully rebuild everything that al-Zee destroyed, as soon as possible. It was good for morale.

Hector drove onto the tarmac and right up to the wing of the private jet. He pressed the door-open button and said nothing.

"Eric, everything depends on you finding the Prime Influencer. I can stall, but not forever."

"No pressure," said Mackey, more to himself.

Two guards pulled the Avatar out of the hydrocab. A third aimed his gun between Mackey's eyes. Hector held up a hand and told him in Arabic to stand down. The men briefly exchanged heated words that Mackey couldn't understand. His heart didn't stop pounding until Hector dropped him off two blocks from his house and drove away. The relief was temporary. Everything depended on him, but deep down he knew the task was impossible, either because there really was no such thing as the Prime Influencer or because the pattern was too subtle for his algorithms to detect. That night he sat home alone in the dark, thinking of his co-workers who had died, how he almost died himself, and the Avatar's programming challenge. He rotated each of the horrible thoughts in his mind until exhaustion overtook him.

AVATAR AND AL-ZEE
DISCUSS THE
MAGICIAN

The Avatar slept for most of the flight, waking up blindfolded. The sounds and smells on the way to al-Zee's underground compound were different from the last time. It was a new route. When the blindfold was removed, the Avatar blinked back the excess light until his eyes adjusted. Al-Zee was standing in front of him, waving the guards out of the room. "Do you know why you're here?" he asked with an unmistakable undertone of anger.

"By now you have found a magician," said the Avatar. "And something happened that you can't explain."

"Who is the magician? Does he work for you? For Cruz?"

"The magician is just a magician. He works for himself, I assume."

"I don't believe in coincidences," said al-Zee over his shoulder, his back to the Avatar to conceal how shaken he was.

"Do you believe that you could flip a coin twice and have it come up heads both times?" asked the Avatar.

"I believe in *simple* coincidences. I'm talking about the most unlikely sort."

"For example," the Avatar tried to clarify, "you believe God must exist because it's too much of a coincidence that the universe is so perfectly designed."

"That is obviously true. What is your point?"

"Cruz and you are true believers. You will be gambling billions of lives on your beliefs. How certain are you that you're right?"

"Completely certain," snapped al-Zee. "Allah does not side with infidels."

"Have you seen anything recently that would make you question your perceptions?" asked the Avatar.

"You know I have," said al-Zee. "You knew I would see a magician. How did you know?"

"I didn't know for sure. But I used a technique from hypnosis to make it likely."

"I was not hypnotized," said al-Zee.

"You weren't in a trance, that's true. But last time we spoke, I put a suggestion in your head about a magician, and that changed how your mind filtered your perceptions. Magicians have worked your streets for years, but until now you paid no attention. The brain can only handle so much information, so it automatically ignores what it judges to be irrelevant. Once the suggestion of a magician was in your mind, it seemed relevant, so your brain no longer ignored it."

"Perhaps that explains why I saw him. It does not explain how he made a camel disappear in front of me and reappear in my washroom, only to disappear again the next moment. How was that done?"

"Were you watching him the whole time the camel disappeared?"

"I was standing right in front of him."

"Were you distracted by anything?"

"No."

The Avatar said nothing, waiting. Al-Zee paused, then corrected: "Yes. A messenger told me that you had escaped. I must have looked away. But that doesn't explain how the camel got in my washroom, much less how it got out."

"That part is the simplest. The camel was never in your washroom."

"I saw it with my own eyes."

"Like all great leaders, you are a true believer. You don't believe for the sake of convenience or tradition in the way that ordinary people often do. You literally see and hear things that other people do not see and hear. You are highly suggestible by nature. When you saw the magician, and were confused at how I predicted it, the confusion put you in a highly suggestible frame of mind. The brain resists confusion. It will create delusions to fill the gaps. In this case your brain tried to solve the puzzle of the disappearing camel. The beast had to go someplace."

"You would have me believe that I imagined a camel?"

"You believe that Allah talks to you."

"*That* is different."

"If it were *completely* different, you wouldn't have brought me here," said the Avatar. "You're having doubts about your perceptions."

"I know what I saw. And I know what I heard."

"Did you see the camel up close?"

"I heard its hooves. I smelled it. And I saw its head in the shadows."

"You heard *something* while you were in a suggestible frame of mind, while you were wondering where the camel went. Your brain interpreted the sounds and smells and even sights to solve your uncertainty."

"Are you calling me crazy?"

"Most people believe they've seen at least one ghost in their life. Their false memories are created the same way as yours. They are in a suggestible frame of mind, perhaps frightened, or overwhelmed with grief at the passing of a relative, and they hear a noise, detect a smell, feel a breeze, and their brains create details that don't exist. A curtain becomes an apparition of a young girl. A reflection in glass becomes a disembodied spirit. What happened to you is a lesson in the fragility of your perception. I wanted you to experience it firsthand."

"How do you know what you know?"

"Talent is unevenly distributed."

"And you are so . . . *talented* . . . that you can see the world more clearly than everyone else?" al-Zee asked sarcastically.

"Consider that each person has a different understanding of the world. Logically, only one of those people can have the most accurate understanding. Surely that one person exists, just as there exists a strongest human, one who is the best at math, and another who can leap the highest. For every skill, someone has the most."

"What is your game? What do you want of me? Just tell me so I can be done with you. I have important things to do."

"Come to Basel, Switzerland, tomorrow at noon. There is someone I want you to meet."

Al-Zee looked at the Avatar and shook his head. There was so much wrong with this request that it was hard to know where to begin. First, it would be difficult for someone of his profile to travel unnoticed outside the Muslim-controlled countries, especially now. War was about to break out. He needed to focus all his energies on the conflict. He barely knew the Avatar, and he knew nothing about the person he was supposed to meet. It was an absurd request. Completely out of line.

"You know I won't go. Why do you ask anyway?"

"I know you have doubts about the war."

"And this will eliminate my doubts?"

"It will increase your doubts."

"Who is this mysterious stranger I should meet?" al-Zee asked, shaking his head.

"If I told you, then you wouldn't go."

"I have had enough. You are a distraction."

Al-Zee opened the door and motioned for the guards to take the Avatar away. "This time make sure he doesn't escape."

"The Hotel Euler, in Basel, at noon tomorrow. I will meet you there," said the Avatar over his shoulder as he was led away.

"I should have known you were crazy," muttered al-Zee.

That night, al-Zee welcomed the knock on his bedroom quarters door at 2:00 A.M. He couldn't sleep, not even close. This emergency, whatever it was, would provide a reason to be awake.

Being awake wouldn't seem so bad if he had a reason. "What is it?" snapped al-Zee at the breathless messenger.

"He's gone."

"Who's gone?"

"The old man. The guards just . . . let him go. They can't explain why."

Al-Zee ripped the covers off his bed and stood.

The messenger explained, "We are looking everywhere for him. He can't escape."

"Stop looking," said al-Zee.

"Stop looking?"

"And tell my aides I'm going to Switzerland tomorrow."

SUMMIT IN
SWITZERLAND

Even on the brink of global war, al–Zee's diplomatic flights were permitted. No one needed to know who was onboard the small jet. Al-Zee's security people were apoplectic. It was insane to fly to a Christian country right now, even a nonaligned one, especially to meet a stranger recommended by a nut. It was foolish in every way.

Al-Zee fumed the entire trip. He hated the Avatar for screwing with his mind. Or was it his own fault for letting him burrow in? Why was this old man so persuasive? Al-Zee convinced himself that it had been so many years since anyone challenged his opinions that the Avatar had put him off balance, made him doubt. And this was the worst time for doubt. How did the old man keep escaping? The escapes conferred credibility, in some way that al-Zee couldn't reconcile.

It wasn't uncommon for Arabs in traditional garb to travel to Switzerland, to take advantage of either the scenery or the banking. Al-Zee and his security force drew almost no attention as they traveled from the airport to the hotel. There were no published pictures of al-Zee, so no one took a second look. He was one of the most famous people in the history of the world, but outside his personal contacts no one really knew what he looked like. His security guards scanned the hotel lobby, expecting the worst. They were armed and ready for anything. All they saw was the Avatar's small body in an oversize chair, napping. Al-Zee approached the sleeping Avatar and cleared his throat, waiting to be noticed. It didn't work. After an awkward pause, a bodyguard tapped the Avatar on the shoulder to wake him.

"Ah, you're here," said the Avatar, still half asleep. "The other is already in the room."

"And just who is the other?" asked al-Zee, in a worsening mood.

"If I told you, you wouldn't believe me. It's easier to show you. Come with me."

The Avatar led the suspicious group to an elevator and pressed the button for the top floor. The ride was unpleasant for everyone but the Avatar, who seemed entirely happy to be there. When they entered the penthouse suite, a large figure, alone, was gazing out the window. He turned and looked at al-Zee, not liking what he saw. Expressions of horror crossed the faces of al-Zee's bodyguards, and they reached for their weapons. The Avatar casually walked between the nervous guests.

"General Cruz, I would like you to meet al-Zee," said the Avatar with a nonchalance that seemed inappropriate to the occasion. Al-Zee and Cruz stared at each other, both in disbelief.

"How do I know that's al-Zee?" asked Cruz.

"How do you know you can't flap your wings and fly?" asked the Avatar. "Some things you just know."

"I am al-Zee. What is this trick?"

"It's just the two of you," said the Avatar, gesturing for his guests to sit. "The bodyguards will have to leave. General Cruz's men are already gone."

Wanting to appear unworried, al-Zee motioned to his guards to leave. They performed a quick search of the closets, bathroom, and hiding spaces before stepping outside.

"I'll be damned," said Cruz, still in amazement.

"I expect that you will be," answered al-Zee.

"Did you know I was going to be here?" asked Cruz.

"No. Did you know about me?"

"No."

Al-Zee and Cruz both looked at the Avatar.

"Well?" asked Cruz. "What the hell good do you think this is going to do?"

The Avatar moved forward in his chair and opened a drawer on the side of the table. He removed a wooden chess set and placed it between the men.

"Is this your idea of a joke?" asked al-Zee.

"Tell me, al-Zee, do you believe God is directing you?" asked the Avatar, arranging the chess pieces on the board.

"Yes, I do."

"And you, General Cruz, do you believe God is guiding your decisions?"

"He is."

"Then I offer a solution to avoid war: one game of chess. Let God give wisdom to whomever he favors. Winner takes all. No bloodshed, no war. The loser must convert to the winner's religion and try to convince his followers to do the same."

"This is nonsense. History is not decided by games," said al-Zee.

Cruz stared at the chessboard while the Avatar arranged the pieces. The general played at the Grand Master level. There was a certain appeal to playing one game of chess, as crazy as it sounded. He knew it wouldn't avert war, but the idea of humiliating al-Zee before the start of action seemed like good psychological warfare.

"I'm in," said Cruz.

"Ridiculous," protested al-Zee.

"Are you afraid God will let you lose?" taunted Cruz.

"God does not use chess to express his will."

"You're both men of your word," interjected the Avatar. "If you agree here and now that this game will determine the outcome of the war, then it is so. You have the power to make this game God's instrument for avoiding the deaths of innocents."

The Avatar stood and bowed to each of the leaders. "I will leave you now and be back in one hour."

"You know we aren't going to agree to this, don't you?" asked al-Zee.

"Yes, I do know that," said the Avatar while walking to the door.

"Then why are you doing it?" asked Cruz.

"I think you mean, why is *God* doing this?" said the Avatar while closing the door behind him.

Cruz and al-Zee sat across from each other, wondering what to do. They were the most powerful people in the history of the world, but alone in this hotel room they looked quite ordinary, and they felt that way.

"No deal," said al-Zee. "I know your background. I know you are an expert at this game. I see now that the Avatar is working for you."

"I wish he were."

An awkward silence fell on the room. The two had so much to talk about that neither knew where to start.

"One game," said al-Zee. "But it is not binding on the war."

Cruz smiled and took a pawn off the board, hid it behind his back, then produced two closed fists. Al-Zee picked the left hand, the one with the hidden pawn, earning him the white pieces and the opening move.

Five minutes into the game, when Cruz had expected to be finished, he found himself on the defensive. He realized that al-Zee had been bluffing. He was not only proficient at the game but an equal to Cruz, perhaps better. Cruz had been totally suckered, and that thought played on his mind, affecting his confidence, exactly as al-Zee knew it would.

"It was a stupid idea," Cruz said, the first conversation since the opening move.

"Ridiculous," agreed al-Zee.

"But I don't know *why* it's stupid," said Cruz. "If we agreed to play chess instead of making war, that would be God's will."

"That would be *our* will, not God's," said al-Zee while moving his rook to attack position.

"That's just it. How do you know what is *your* will and what is *God's* will?"

Al-Zee looked up from the game and studied the face of his opponent.

"You can feel it in your heart when it is real," said al-Zee.

"But how can we both be right if we're feeling opposite things?"

"Your heart is corrupted by evil. You have been misled."

"How do you know that *you* aren't the one misled? It seems that way to me."

"Checkmate," said al-Zee, positioning his bishop.

Cruz just stared at the board, fuming inside, trying not to show it. He stood and walked toward the window, as if to say it meant nothing. He wasn't doing a good job of it.

"You are so sure of your rightness," said al-Zee to Cruz's back. "Your huge armies, so invincible. Your arrogance will be your undoing. God will make an example of you that will last the ages."

Al-Zee stood. For the first time, Cruz considered that he could lose the war. That thought had never before crossed his mind. It had always been a question of how long it would take, or how many casualties each side would have. But he had never entertained the notion of losing. He had been as sure of his chess superiority an hour ago. His sense of certainty and destiny was being tested. Yes, he thought, it must be a test.

"I know who you are," growled Cruz, turning to face al-Zee. "You are the one he warned us about: the dark one. You test my faith, but you will not succeed. You cannot succeed. God won't allow it."

The Avatar entered the room, halting the conversation, to the relief of both men. The Avatar looked down at the chess game, absorbing what had happened, and smiled.

"You have a result," he said.

"It means nothing," said Cruz. "It's a game."

"It's a sign," said al-Zee. "A sign of things to come."

"I have a proposition for both of you," said the Avatar. "A proposition to avoid the war and give both sides everything they need."

Cruz and al-Zee said nothing. Neither wanted to seem eager to avoid the fight. But their silence signaled their willingness to listen.

"My idea is that General Cruz surrender immediately, unconditionally."

Cruz laughed. "Your ideas keep getting better and better," he said.

"What is it that *you* want?" the Avatar asked al-Zee.

"Dignity," replied al-Zee. "I want justice. I want vengeance. I want my people to have the pride that has been denied them by centuries of infidels such as General Cruz."

"And what do *you* want, General Cruz?" asked the Avatar.

"Security. I want these bastards to stop killing people."

"So there you have it," said the Avatar. "You want different things, and the things you want are in the power of the other to give, free and clear."

"That's a great idea if I want to be a Muslim," scoffed Cruz.

"Would you want to convert him?" asked the Avatar to al-Zee.

"I wouldn't waste my time," said al-Zee. "I prefer that he burn in hell."

"And do you want to control his land?" asked the Avatar.

"I want only to control Muslim land," replied al-Zee.

"That's bullshit." Cruz spit. "You'd do the same thing to us that you did to Israel. You'd breed until you controlled every country. And then you'd demand to have Muslim rule. You wouldn't stop until you owned it all."

"Imagine that future for a minute, General," encouraged the Avatar. "Let's say you have a growing Muslim population in one of your democratic NATO countries. They have the same access to voting, education, and job opportunities as everyone else in the country. Is that how terrorists are bred?"

"You're saying they'd get fat and happy?"

"I'm asking if you can imagine any other possibility. Surely you can point to examples where fairly treated, middle-class people have pushed for revolution."

Cruz was a student of history. He knew that there were no such examples, and that revolution grows from oppression and shortage, not fairness and democracy. He backed away from a losing argument and tried another approach. "I can't take that risk," he said. "You might be right. They might get seduced by leisure and decide to sit on their asses and drink Starbucks coffee instead of overthrowing the government. But I can't take that chance. And besides, how the hell would I explain to my people that I was surrendering to a weaker power?"

"Is that really the problem, General? You don't know how to *explain* the best solution? Why not let the results speak for themselves? Try it and wait a few months to see if the bombings stop. See if the terror cells disband."

Cruz looked at al-Zee and approached him. "Look me in the eye. Tell me that if I . . . *surrendered* . . . you wouldn't keep attacking. Tell me you wouldn't ask for anything."

"I would ask for an apology," said al-Zee.

"Apology?! Apology!?" Cruz yelled with two different intonations to make his point. "You bomb the crap out of us for years, you overrun Israel, our ally, and slaughter the citizens, and you want an apology from *us*?!"

"It is not what I *want*. It is what I *need* to stop the violence." Al-Zee looked at the Avatar and continued. "I accept your plan. I will agree to end all violence in return for an unconditional surrender and an apology for a thousand years of indignities. I give my word—"

The General interrupted. "That's easy for you to say. You win without a fight—a fight you know you would lose. You give up nothing. But you ask me to humble myself to a bunch of thugs and terrorists."

"How many lives is your dignity worth, General?" asked the Avatar. "Does it come to this? Your pride is worth two billion lives? Is that how Jesus would have handled it?"

"That's not what I'm saying!" yelled Cruz. "This is total bull-shit. The man is a terrorist. He's not going to keep his word. There's no deal to be had."

"It's simple to test," noted the Avatar. "If nothing blows up, he has kept his word. If not, then you still have the same army you had before. And you would know for sure that reasoning with him is futile, and so would the rest of the world. You'd have pub-lic opinion on your side in a way you've never had. You'd come out ahead no matter what happens."

"Why not ask al-Zee to surrender? If he stops blowing up stuff, this whole thing goes away," said Cruz.

"He would be killed in minutes, by his own followers," responded the Avatar. "It would not solve the root problem of Muslim pride. It would only worsen it. Another leader would take his place."

Cruz paced the floor in front of the window, looking out, thinking how to respond. He turned to the Avatar. "You know I'm not going to agree to this."

"Yes, I know."

"Then why go through all the trouble?"

"Short answer or long answer?" asked the Avatar.

"The short one."

"I need time. As long as you two are here, with me, the war is postponed."

"Time for what?" al-Zee asked.

"To find the one who can stop the war," said the Avatar.

"Only *we* can stop the war," said Cruz.

"No," said the Avatar. "You have just proven that you don't have the power."

"And someone else does?" asked al-Zee, annoyed by the suggestion.

"You should hope so," said the Avatar.

Cruz and al-Zee didn't shake hands or acknowledge each other again. Both felt that there was nothing more to say, so they gathered their people and left. For the rest of the day, both men pondered the opportunity they had let pass. Doubt turned to anger, and anger turned to battle planning.

It was war.

WAR BEGINS

Mackey's apartment was a monument to bad home design. He was a man who lived in his head. Clothing and furniture were beyond his interest, and it showed. He was wearing pajama bottoms and a sweatshirt when the Avatar arrived. He hadn't shaved in days. His eyes were puffy and pooched, lined with gray.

"I bought you a day," said the Avatar.

"It doesn't matter. It can't be done."

"It can. I know it can."

"It's too late, anyway," said Mackey, punching up the CNN web page.

"Cruz has already deployed. He's knocking out al-Zee's communications infrastructure. We're in it now. Even if I found this magical person you're looking for, it's too late. The time for talking is over."

"Come with me to H-Two. You'll be safe there while you work."

"I'm not leaving here," said Mackey. "I have a gas mask. And they'll never let me into H-Two. My brother-in-law is a Muslim. Cruz would have me shot on the spot."

"Do you have plastic for the windows?" asked the Avatar.

"Yes, of course. I'll be fine. But I can't work with you bugging me."

An explosion sounded outside, then another, then a string of them. Some hit nearby, others were farther away. Al-Zee was already retaliating.

The Avatar wished Mackey luck and headed outside to his waiting hydrocab. Hector was gone, but his cab remained, with a note. It said: "Good luck, Mr. Avatar. The Cab is yours. May Allah help us both survive.—Ali." The Avatar got into the cab and drove toward H2. He turned on the radio to follow the war's progress and to pick the least perilous route.

The city was on fire. Over the past five years, al-Zee's cells had placed explosives in dozens of the largest buildings in the city and on the access bridges and roads into the metropolitan area. The city was isolated and on fire, but everyone knew it was only the first phase. Al-Zee's signature attack involved simultaneous events and always two phases. It was psychological warfare. When you thought the worst was over, he proved it was not.

The drones, laden with biological weapons, hadn't yet been launched. Already the city was an obstacle course of fire equipment, debris, and hysterical crowds. The Avatar's first job—it seemed so long ago—had been delivering packages. He still had an instinct for picking the best routes and the fastest moving lanes. And now that he was a fully aware Avatar, his driving skills bordered on psychic. He evaded debris and pedestrians as if he knew they were coming before he saw them, and in fact he did. His mind was a swirl of overlapping patterns. Never before had he felt so many patterns, like Venn diagrams, intersecting, rippling, dissipating, and re-creating. His mind was processing thousands of inputs, then millions, then billions. He could no longer feel his hands on the wheel or his foot on the accelerator. He belonged to the activity, a part of it, surfing its ripples, moving into openings before they formed, speeding and slowing according to some unfathomable assemblage of rules and patterns in his mind.

As he zigzagged through traffic and other obstacles, he thought of his objective, to stop the war. He had failed. The war was on. He was confused. How could it be happening when he was so sure he could stop it, so sure he was supposed to stop it, so sure it was hard-coded into his future? He hoped that maybe there was still time to stop the worst of it, but that thought evaporated with the sound of a drone passing low over his head. The second wave had begun. The streets were filled with pedestrians, the media's cameras were rolling, and the biological terror was upon them.

H2 had limited space for nonmilitary people. In case of emergency it was designed to house diplomats and politicians who lived nearby. It was the safest place in the metropolitan area. The Avatar had negotiated his own space at H2 ahead of time. Cruz had agreed, because although the Avatar creeped him out, he still seemed to know a lot. And that could come in handy.

The Avatar got in line behind a hundred people hoping to get into H2. There were mothers and children, hydrocab drivers and businesspeople. Guards worked the line, trying to find people who were preauthorized. One of the guards recognized the Avatar from his first visit and asked his name. Finding him on the list, the guard ushered the Avatar to the front of the line and into the gate, past the desperate curses of those left behind. The Avatar looked at the faces in line before entering. He knew they would all be dead in hours, if they were lucky. In days if they weren't. He had failed. The full weight of his failure was building inside him, corrosive and thick. The survivors would be emerging to a ruined world. Some would survive, but none would prosper. Not in this lifetime. The Avatar felt rage, an emotion he had not felt since he ascended to Avatar. Or had he ascended to anything at all? Maybe there was no such thing as an Avatar. Maybe he was insane after all.

How can a man know whether he has more awareness than anyone else, and not more mental problems? He wondered how much of the past year was even real. Was today real? Could it all be a dream? It seemed so much like a product of his imagination; his imagination was so good that the distinction between his thoughts and reality was hard to sort out. His doubts and the weight of failure converged to form a sharp pain in the Avatar's chest. For the first time in years, the patterns in his mind vanished. There was nothing. He just existed. His mind was quiet while his torso thumped in rhythmic agony. He couldn't *feel* the people around him as easily as before. He could only see them and hear them. This is what failure feels like, he thought.

H2 was chaotic, loud, bustling. Highly trained military men and women focused on their jobs, knowing that their loved ones outside the protected walls would probably die that day. There was no security inside H2 to prevent people from roaming freely. Checking credentials would be too much of a distraction. The Avatar's arms and legs felt heavy. The sleeplessness of the past week had started to catch up with him. He was hungry now too. Starving. He didn't remember the last time he had eaten. There was an unpleasant calmness about failure, he thought. His mind was released from big thoughts. It was too late. Now it was about survival, eating, sleeping, and staying sane. He wondered how he could have been so wrong. His mentor, the prior Avatar, had predicted this war. Since then, he had been preparing for it, learning everything he could, becoming more aware, sharpening his thinking skills. In the end, it wasn't enough. War was upon the world. Or had he imagined the prior Avatar? Was it the day he became aware or the day he went insane? He was only sure that he couldn't know the answer to that question. No one can know if they are deluded. That's just the way it works.

The Avatar wandered to the officers' lounge, where a crowd of civilians—mostly politicians—was gathering. Everyone was on the phone, talking to those left behind, assuming it would be the last time most of them spoke with each other.

The Avatar's attention moved to the corner of the room, where a string of curses emerged in a familiar voice. A pink-haired woman jabbed at the keypad of her phone, held it to her ear, cursed and jabbed again. The Avatar approached her, drawn to the only familiar face amidst the horror.

"I didn't expect to see you here," he said.

"I have connections, Captain," said Stacey, still jabbing at her keypad. "Crap! I grabbed the wrong phone before I evacuated. I can't reach my husband. This one is filtered to someone else's call list. Crap, crap, crap! He doesn't even know I'm here. I got him approved to get into H–Two, but he doesn't know it. He's probably in the safe room at the house, trying to call me, but he can't get through to me either."

The Avatar's head pounded as he listened, knowing that her husband would be lost within hours. The war had been an abstraction to the Avatar until now. Here was a specific person who would die because he had failed. Failure made breathing difficult.

"Do you think I should start believing in God now, Captain?" Stacey said, still fiddling uselessly with her phone, as if trying it over and over again would help.

"I don't know what anyone should think right now," said the Avatar, resigned, as he let his back slide down the wall until he was sitting against it.

Stacey sat down next to him. "Is this how you figured it would turn out?" she asked.

"No," muttered the Avatar, looking at the floor.

"Tell me *your* version, Captain. How was this supposed to all work out? I need to hear a story. Make me think of something else."

Stacey closed her phone and set it on the floor next to her.

"Do you really want to know?"

"Yes. Get my mind off of what's happening. I know you have stories. I can tell by looking at you."

The Avatar paused, collected his breath, sighed, took another breath, and began. "About fourteen billion years ago, there existed only one particle."

"That's all? One speck?"

"One speck, as you say. Imagine, it pops into existence and in an instant it is gone, then the process repeats, like a pulse. While it exists, it is alone, singular, and complete. It can't be divided. It is the smallest piece of reality. While it is gone, time doesn't exist, because time is nothing but the motion of things compared to other things, and when nothing exists, time is meaningless."

"You're crazy. I like this. Keep talking."

"This speck, this one indivisible bit of reality, is perfect. It can't be destroyed because nothing exists to destroy it. It has no unfulfilled needs. It is everywhere, because it alone exists. There is nothing outside it or over it or inside it. Nothing has dominion over it."

"So the speck is like God or something? Is that what you're saying?"

"In a universe where nothing but the speck exists, the speck is almighty."

"That's not too almighty if you ask me. A speck can't think," Stacey countered. "The speck is just a speck."

"Thinking is only useful for imperfect creatures. Humans think to survive. We think to predict the future. The speck is better than that. It doesn't need to think to survive. It has no need for insecurity or fear. It is perfect, timeless, and complete."

"It can't even talk. It's just a speck. That's not exactly omnipotent," returned Stacey.

"What does it mean to say you have power to do something that you have no motivation to do? Power that will never be used is not power at all. It is nothing but a human concept. The speck has everything it needs. It has no frailties, desires, or motivations. It simply exists, and thus it is perfect."

"This story better get better. The speck is cool, but if it becomes a movie, I'm not paying to see it."

"It gets better."

"So how'd all the other stuff get here? Did the speck create it? Or were there lots of specks?"

"It is meaningless to ask if the speck is alone or part of an infinite number of identical specks because only one existed at a time and then disappeared. There were only two conditions: existing and not existing. To a computer programmer, it was like a one and a zero. That is the most basic pattern."

"That almost makes sense, but not really. Keep going."

"Then, *two* specks popped into existence in the same place."

"Why?"

"Change is the fundamental nature of the universe, and so there is no answer to why. You might try to understand it by saying the speck was curious or that it wanted a challenge, but a speck is not burdened by human motivations."

"Okay, whatever, so then what? One speck had to get out of the way for the other one?"

"Yes. And the rhythm of existence was broken. A chain reaction started, with speck after speck coming into existence on top of one another, each one needing to move to unoccupied space, creating all the matter in the universe as it went."

"That second speck was like an evil twin. Look at all the crap it caused."

"Yes, you could imagine the first speck to be perfect, and ordered. The second speck caused chaos and motion. Everything bad that ever happens is because of the second speck. It has spawned many metaphors, chief among them: Satan."

"So now what, the good speck and the bad speck are duking it out?"

"In a manner, yes. There are two overwhelming forces in the world. One is chaos; the other is order. God—the original singular speck—is forming again. He's gathering together his bits— we call it gravity. And in the process he is becoming self-aware to defeat chaos, to defeat evil if you will, to battle the devil. But something has gone terribly wrong."

"Yeah, the war."

"Not just that. I felt I was supposed to help God become conscious, so the war could be avoided. But it didn't happen. Now I suspect that you are right: I'm crazy after all."

"What do you mean by 'conscious'?"

"The Internet was, I thought, God's central nervous system, connecting all the thinking humans, so that one good thought anywhere could be available everywhere. The head would know what the feet were feeling. It would be an upper consciousness, above what the human beings that composed it would understand."

"We have an Internet. That already happened."

"Not completely. The war on terrorism stopped it from being what it was trying to be. There are too many restrictions now. People only see what the government wants them to see. Everything else is filtered. Even the phone system is crippled. You can only call approved people. God's central nervous system is incomplete. And without that, I believe the war is unstoppable. Chaos will win."

"The bad speck wins? This story sucks, if you don't mind me saying."

Stacey picked up her phone and tried dialing again. Nothing.

"Frickin' speck."

MACKEY
WRITES CODE

Mackey was sweating. The plastic for his safe room was taped up, he had a supply of food and water, and his television reported the progress of al-Zee's attacks on the city. He tried to work on his laptop while reporters described the war outside his windows. He couldn't ignore the Avatar's challenge of using his database skills to find the one most influential person alive, the one that could change all this, and maybe stop it. He had serious doubts that such a person could exist. He had even more doubts that the database held enough clues for him to find that one special person. But he didn't doubt his skills. If it was possible, he would do it.

Mackey shifted into his serious programming mode, a state in which he didn't feel hungry, scared, hot, or tired. Mentally he left his body and inhabited the program. He imagined the computer code as physical objects, with himself in miniature, looking around, checking the structure. It was like a pinball machine with the control of the program being the ball as it moved through each line of the program from top to bottom, being redirected by flippers and banks and obstacles, each with specific rules established by

Mackey's code. When the pinball went awry, he snapped back to his normal size and typed some adjustments, then tried again.

This was undisciplined, undocumented, no-rules programming. Mackey didn't need flowcharts, staff meetings, or user requirements. He had been writing computer code since he was six. He could program as fast as he could type, over a hundred words a minute. He could code while exhausted. He could code in any mood, in any place. His cockiness was not misplaced. He thought he might be the best that ever lived and he had a habit of mentioning that to his co-workers. They thought he was a jerk, but no one doubted the claim. He was the main architect of the GIC database and a holder of eighty-three patents. He didn't just *write* code, he invented it as he went.

All the obvious approaches hadn't worked. He knew they wouldn't work before trying them, but he thought that in failure a better idea would emerge. Maybe something that didn't work would suggest a better approach. It wasn't much of a hope, but it was all he had. He was working on pure instinct, writing code by reflex, sometimes having to read it after he typed it just to know what he wrote. The methodical method had failed. Now he was poking around in the dark, hoping to get lucky, although he would never confess to luck. It was a "managed luck," he liked to think, a process of eliminating the impossible until the possible revealed itself. It was all dark alleys and deep wells. Poke and test.

Mackey wrote some programs to help him write other programs, leveraging his considerable genius. His computer screen filled with dots of different colors, each indicating a different type of data, swirling and fluid, like dirty water. He combined code used for DNA analysis with code for fluid dynamics and created subroutines that literally evolved, changing on their own, according to the data they encountered. Like sharks in an ocean, the subroutines were attracted to the smell of blood miles away and moved toward it. This was crazy code—brilliant, unpredictable, and almost thinking.

Mackey felt his first physical sensation in an hour, a chill that ran up his back when he realized what he had done. He had created a digital ecosystem that was crossbreeding, creating virtual creatures to hunt for the Prime Influencer. It was happening at light speed. Virtual species in Mackey's code world evolved, lived, hunted, and sometimes got devoured in nanoseconds by more capable digital entities. Mackey sat back and watched as the forms of creatures flashed on his screen, each one different from the last. The virtual creatures lived off the database as if it were the Earth. They resided on it, consumed it, then died and became part of it. Mackey had found a program that multiplied his own intelligence a billion times, then a billion times a billion times. He was in awe of his own work, watching it process, build, virtually live.

And then it stopped.

Mackey stared at the screen for a few minutes, hoping it would restart. When it didn't, he checked the run logs. Some of his digital creatures had evolved to have human characteristics. And they had just annihilated all life in his program, including their own.

Mackey slunk back against the wall of his safe room. The explosions were getting nearer. The television reported that drones were spraying an unidentified chemical over the city that was so highly aerosol it resisted floating to the ground. It just hung in the air and spread sideways. Anyone who was exposed died within an hour. Early reports were that the chemical had one quality that the Homeland Security department hadn't anticipated.

It melted plastic.

A TV reporter described how plastic would turn brown before melting from the airborne chemical. Mackey looked at the perimeter of his safe room. One corner, covering a ceiling vent, was already brown.

There wouldn't be time for another try. He was done. Mackey felt a calm sense of detachment about his impending death. He hoped it would be quick. He felt oddly curious about what it would feel like the moment before expiration. But mostly he needed to talk to someone. He needed to make some calls. He would call his parents and his brothers, to lie and say he was fine. He wanted to hear their voices one more time. Mackey picked up his phone and dialed his parents. A message blinked "Unauthorized Call." Checking the serial code on the back of the phone, Mackey knew he had the right device, and it was authorized for calls to his family. There was only one explanation. The military must have shut down all personal calling, to limit the spread of panic and control the flow of information about the war. Mackey's television set went black.

The plastic on his ceiling was flaking off, raining large bits of brown debris on the floor. Mackey knew the end was near.

"I just want to make a phone call," he muttered to himself.

BLACK FORCE

Cruz's soldiers rarely saw who they were killing. It was war at a distance. Battle platforms swept enemy missiles out of the sky before they could reach Christian Alliance battleships. Smart missiles destroyed all of al-Zee's antiaircraft capabilities in the first hours of the war, circling patiently until radar locked on to them, then diving toward the sources, obliterating them. Missiles and fighter jets did the rest, delivering massive destruction to targets that had no specific description. Pilots no longer needed to know that their targets were ammo dumps or bridges. The central battle computer assigned targets and programmed the GPS systems of the pilots on the fly, making adjustments in real time based on drone surveillance of the battlefield. Pilots didn't need to know what they were bombing or why, and Cruz counted on that fact to pursue his goal of annihilation.

A few hours earlier, Cruz and Waters had sat in front of a computer that presented all conceivable battle options. Every target was listed, its military value scored. Cruz could select targets and click the Reforecast button to see how any particular plan would turn out, within a reasonable degree of certainty. Once a plan was selected, the specific orders would be sent automatically to the computers and GPS systems of every member of the military, along with timing details. No one but Waters knew that Cruz had chosen Select All to destroy the entire military and civilian population of the Muslim world. And no one *could* know, until it was too late to change it. Reporters weren't allowed in the battle area. Television and radio signals in al-Zee's territory were jammed electronically before the first missile was fired. Cruz ordered all phone number databases to be shut down, disabling the system worldwide. An independent multinational group out of Switzerland controlled the global phone number database, theoretically outside the jurisdiction of any government, but they weren't prepared to argue with Cruz. They did as they were told.

Extermination had begun. A thick rain of missiles streaked through the sky and landed on hospitals, schools, bridges, homes, mosques, businesses, and military targets. The missile crews and jet pilots didn't know what they were blowing up or why. They assumed that military intelligence had detected secret underground bunkers and weapons sites under civilian areas. Everyone understood that there would be civilian casualties. No one questioned why entire blocks—eventually entire cities—were being annihilated. Everyone did his job as if it were nothing more than delivering packages. For Cruz's side, war was abstract.

Cruz's Black Force, the elite team trained to assassinate al-Zee, easily penetrated Lower Qadum's defenses, with the help of an insider who mistakenly believed that collaboration would spare his family. Dressed in local garb and led by Captain Troy Spencer, Black Force worked its way through the streets of Lower Qadum, toward al-Zee's living quarters. Spencer tried not to think about the uselessness of this assignment. He knew that killing al-Zee would have no impact on the war. In fact, it might be harder to stop the fighting once the only person who could agree to peace was dead. The rumor in Black Force was that this mission was personal, that Cruz wanted al-Zee dead, not just trapped in Lower Qadum for his lifetime. It wasn't their job to ponder the moral or strategic implications of what they did. They were too well trained.

A packet of C4 eliminated an outer wall of al-Zee's compound while another simultaneously took out his electrical system and backup generators. Black Force entered the breach, equipped with silent firearms and night-vision glasses. They neutralized al-Zee's personal bodyguards with clinical efficiency. The frightened-looking man at the center of this protection sat alone, grasping a Koran to his chest and praying aloud. A bullet ended his prayer. Spencer photographed the corpse for verification and took a lock of hair for DNA analysis later.

ASSASSINATION
ATTEMPT

The Avatar's sense of failure was turning into depression. His body felt heavy and lifeless. Stacey was talking to him, but he couldn't hear her anymore. He was lost in a replay of his life. How could he have ever imagined he was the chosen one? He had skills that other people didn't have; that was clear. He could see patterns and he knew things without knowing how he knew. But it was a far leap from that to say he knew the nature of God and the future of reality. Was it hubris or stupidity or both? he wondered. He started to think that the whole Avatar delusion must be like a virus, passed on from one mistaken fool to the next. He was unlucky, nothing more. A life of loneliness was wasted.

Or worse, if he really was an Avatar, he had failed. The world would soon be destroyed for all practical purposes. Everything he understood, or thought he understood, about reality was proving wrong. If God existed, and had a plan for reassembling himself, nothing would be able to stop it. In that case the Avatar would *have* to succeed. But he hadn't succeeded, and that meant that his understanding of God was wrong, that his life was an unintentional joke.

A rising murmur in the hallway stirred the Avatar from his spiral of self-loathing. Cruz, Waters, and his aides were approaching, on their way to something important. The nonmilitary people sitting in the hallway stood instinctively as he approached. The Avatar could muster only enough energy to turn his head and watch. Cruz noticed the Avatar and stopped.

"You might as well come with me," said the general. "You'll want to hear this."

"I'll stay here, if that's okay," said the Avatar, too drained to move.

"I'll bring him," said Stacey, pulling the Avatar up by his arm. Cruz just nodded and continued. The Avatar had no fight left in him. He wasn't aware of his own feet as they moved him toward the assembly area.

Cruz took the podium. His aides, Stacey, and the Avatar stood to one side of the standing-room crowd. Anxious military people and a sprinkling of civilian survivors waited to hear anything they could about the fate of the outside world.

Cruz tested the microphone and began. "The war has started. I have authorized my forces to surround the Muslim Territories and prosecute my battle plan. I alone am responsible for the plan of attack, the target choices, and the outcome. I accept the judgment of history for what I am about to do."

"Windbag," whispered Stacey to the Avatar, getting no reaction.

"This will not be a traditional war, where one side surrenders. It is a war of culture, of belief, neither of which *can* surrender.

Our ability to kill each other has exceeded our ability to find common ground. Our only choices are victory or defeat. On your behalf, I choose victory. I have authorized my forces to . . . eliminate . . . al-Zee's supporters."

A civilian in the crowd voiced the question that was on all of their minds. "What do you mean by 'eliminate'?"

Cruz paused. He knew only one way to say it, but the word was stuck in his throat. Once released, it could never be taken back. But the time for ambiguity had passed. The public, what was left of it, would find out eventually. Better it came from him. The word left his mouth like a regurgitated demon.

"Extermination."

The crowd became deathly silent, then stirred as one, whispering, mumbling, shocked, confused. They were part of Cruz's history whether they liked it or not. They would be the people who had let it happen. No one wanted to lose a war, but extermination was going too far. To the ordinary person, and to this crowd in particular, the notion was wrong on every level. It violated their core humanity.

"I know what you're thinking," Cruz continued over the din. "There can be no reason good enough to destroy an entire culture, two billion people, most of which have no quarrel with us. But the alternative is defeat. Their culture is infected with a belief that killing infidels is a ticket to paradise. If we win the war militarily but leave the enemy's beliefs intact, we strengthen them. They will come for us, this time with more powerful weapons of mass destruction. They will not fear death. They will not trade risk for comfort. They would chip away at our economy until we couldn't support our military, then they would destroy us. We must kill the idea. The only way to do that is by eliminating the vessels that carry it."

"How can you be so sure that's the only way?" yelled someone from the crowd.

"God has spoken to me," said Cruz. "His will be done."

Waters snapped his head at the sound of automatic rifle fire. A military man in the crowd had opened fire toward the podium. The soldier shouted a string of obscenities that were mostly incomprehensible until ". . . crazy Hitler bastard! It ends now!"

The podium blocked the chest shot that would have killed Cruz. A second bullet grazed his shoulder and knocked him off his feet, to the relative safety of the floor. The audience grabbed the assailant's arm and subdued him, but they couldn't stop the last few rounds, now unfocused, that launched into the front of the room, tearing through walls, columns, and fixtures. Cruz was on the ground, his sidearm drawn, with Waters on top of him, a human shield. Waters glanced over his shoulder to see that the immediate danger was gone, the traitor in custody. He hustled Cruz toward the side exit, over the body of the Avatar, limp and bleeding, a gaping wound in his chest.

Stacey accompanied the medics as they rushed the Avatar to the internal H2 hospital. They assumed she was a family member, and she didn't try to correct that impression. Cruz and Waters were already there, as doctors dressed Cruz's surface wound. The Avatar was lifted into an adjacent bed. Doctors checked for his pulse and found one, barely. A doctor flipped on the instant MRI to see a three-dimensional image. The bullet was lodged in his heart. Nurses connected an EKG to his head and turned it on.

"Must have been a ricochet. Otherwise it would have gone straight through," said a dark-haired doctor.

"Still, he's done," said a sandy-haired doctor. "The heart is too damaged. Nothing we can do here. And look, there's no brain activity."

Stacey listened and stared. She was wearing a surgical mask, her eyes as big as moons. "You can't let him die!"

"He's already dead, ma'am, for all practical purposes. I'm sorry. We could keep his body working artificially, but without a heart or brain activity there's not much point."

"What about a heart transplant? People get those every day!"

"Not without donors. And we'll need his bed if we have more injuries. If I have to unplug him to keep someone else alive, I'll do it. This is a military hospital. That's just the way it is. And besides, like I said, he has no brain activity."

Stacey's fists were tight as rocks. She could feel her face flushing with an intense urge to punch the doctor. She would never tolerate a pessimistic response at her restaurant, and she didn't appreciate it now. But she couldn't see her way to a better solution. She wouldn't punch anyone yet, but the next few minutes would be a challenge.

"Too bad about the old guy," said Cruz as the doctor finished dressing his wound. "I kind of liked the little fool. Unfortunately this world has no place for dreamers. Life rewards action, not ideas."

Waters felt a burning sensation behind his eyes. For a man who rarely felt anything, this was novel. It wasn't quite a headache, more like a brain ache. He squinted and tried to shake it off, but it only got worse.

MACKEY MAKES A
PHONE CALL

By now, al–Zee assumed, his double would be dead. As a student of history he knew that all impenetrable fortresses had the same weakness—the people who guarded them. Al–Zee had stayed behind in Switzerland after the meeting with Cruz, in a safe house set up for that purpose. He hadn't counted on being completely shut off from communications. But no matter, his cell leaders had their instructions. On day one, the San Francisco metropolitan area would be sprayed with biological agents. If that didn't stop Cruz's attack, Los Angeles was next. Every major city in the Christian Alliance would be destroyed in turn. The cells were in place, autonomous, trained, ready to die. They didn't need communications. All they needed was a calendar.

He would win this war, he told himself, because God wanted him to win. He had never lost before, and that was all the proof he needed that God was on his side against the infidels. Still, he hoped that the war would stop after only a few cities had been destroyed. Surely God did not want dominion over a wasted world. Or maybe that was his plan all along, to purge the nonbelievers and sinners, as he did once before, as with Noah. Al-Zee blushed at the idea that he might be God's latest Noah, the chosen one assigned to restart a cleansed world. But it was hard to deny the facts. It couldn't be a coincidence that he found himself in this position. History would not deny him his place.

Al-Zee's bodyguards had given up trying their phones and Internet connections. But they kept the television on, watching nothing but local news, filled with guesses and speculations about what was happening in the outside world.

At first, most of the world thought there was nothing more worrisome than a communications network problem. They had experienced network outages before, and this seemed similar. After a few hours, some of the older guys dusted off their ham radios, antiques but still workable. They were showing off, as if to say the old ways are better, tongue in cheek. It was fun to find a friendly voice in other ham operators who had the same idea. They gossiped and introduced themselves and joked.

Then they heard from San Francisco. Now it wasn't a game. The ham operators spread the word over long distances, and people spread the word over the short distances. There was panic. The war was on. Everyone knew that this was the big one, that there was no hiding. The looting began immediately. The shooting started soon after, as virtually all adults owned a legal firearm. Would there ever be food again? The grocery stores were hit first, their shelves cleaned by armed neighbors, who in turn were shot by other neighbors for what they had looted. All commerce and traffic stopped. The rule of law evaporated. Civilization in San Francisco dissolved.

Mackey could feel the first choke of al-Zee's deadly gas in his lungs. It had a sickeningly sweet odor. He could feel some stiffness in his extremities that he assumed was the first sign of a complete body lockup. He tapped on his keyboard to free up a program he'd been working on for years, mostly for his own amusement, because it could never be used without risking jail. He had named it the Giver-of-Data program, or GoD for short, because he liked the name. The GoD program snapped to the screen. Mackey checked the boxes labeled "Self-recovery," "Universal," and "Permanent." He laughed as he clicked Execute, and the laugh turned into a cough.

Mackey was the prime architect and keeper of the most comprehensive database on Earth. It knew where people lived, what they bought, what they liked and didn't like, how much they were worth, their medical histories, their families, their friends, their legal and criminal records, a thousand other things, and—most important at the moment—their phone numbers. GoD was like a central nervous system that connected all of the data in the world to all of the phones of the world, a superset of the Universal Phone Directory that Cruz had ordered disabled. GoD spread like a virus, attacking the networks of the telephone companies, all of which had connections to GIC, to which they were required by law to feed their information daily. Once inside the phone companies, GoD overrode their internal directories and pointed to the GIC database for user information. In a matter of minutes, all phones on Earth became unfiltered. Anyone could call anyone. The virus was unstoppable. It reproduced itself and hid copies. It changed its shape and size and characteristics on the fly, making it impossible to identify or capture. It was everywhere. It owned the network. Once unleashed, the program wasn't a physical thing; it was a concept that could not be undone.

Mackey tried to dial his phone, to reach his parents, but his fingers weren't responding well. It was a struggle to press the last few keys. His eyes became unfocused, and his breathing was shallow. His mother's voice came on the line.

"Hello?"

"I love you," he said, then closed his eyes forever.

H2 HOSPITAL ROOM

"Do you know why God spared me and killed the old man, Waters?" asked Cruz, perched on the side of the hospital bed. Waters just looked at him. "Because I'm *right*. God wants me to finish the job, to rid the world of al-Zee and his misguided followers. God did this same thing once before, with Noah. Sometimes you have to clean the barn and start over." Cruz stood and walked over to the Avatar's lifeless body. "This is the part of the barn that God didn't need—the stuff on the ground, if you know what I mean. I'll shovel it out and start over. That's why he picked me, Waters. I know what God wants. Before today I admit that I had some doubts about my plan to eliminate al-Zee's people, but God could have changed that plan today if he wanted. I could be the one with the bullet in my heart instead of this little flesh wound. God is telling me I'm on the right track."

Stacey shuffled down the hallway away from the hospital area. She had lost her only friend inside H2, and she couldn't reach her husband, Mike, on the outside. He was either dead or soon to be. In the next few days, most of civilization would be eliminated. There was no turning back. For the first time in her life, she was out of optimism. Then her phone vibrated. The caller ID showed

"Unknown." She considered not answering it, thinking it was a phantom ring. "Hello?" she said, barely able to voice the word.

"It's Mike. I'm inside H-Two. Where are you?"

"Mike! I thought you didn't make it."

"I talked my way in. I said I knew you. Can you believe that crap? They only let me in because the guards were regulars at your restaurant and you comped their meal one day. They actually remembered that. Where are you?"

"Let me find one of those 'you are here' maps and I'll tell you in a minute."

"I wonder why the phones are working now," said Mike.

"Look at him, Waters," said Cruz, over the Avatar's body. "These machines are keeping his body from rotting, but he's dead. Is he in hell yet, I wonder? Do you go to hell for trying to subvert God's will? He wanted peace, but if God wants war, how can that go unpunished?"

The doctor in attendance tried to ignore what he was overhearing. Waters couldn't look at Cruz. The pounding in his head was increasing. It felt like a dam ready to burst. The sound of Cruz's voice was making it worse.

"It's the weak that die. The undeserving. The unbelievers. God had no need for him. Maybe hell will have a place. Bad things happen to people for a reason, Waters. He did something to piss off God, that's for sure. He looked innocent, but people die for a reason. It's part of the plan."

The dark-haired doctor had heard enough. "Bad things don't happen for a reason. They just happen," he said.

Cruz turned on the doctor. "That's what sinners say, Doc. By now my forces have cut off the major roads out of al-Zee's territory and grounded their air travel. No one gets in or out ever again. And in the next few days, I'll start stomping those rag-wearing bastards like an elephant on an anthill. There *is* a reason. Every one of them picked the wrong religion. They offended God, and God picked me to set things right."

"Most are children," the doctor replied. "What have *they* done?"

"They got born to the wrong parents, that's what. Maybe they had no choice, but they're wrong, and they'll grow up to stay wrong unless I stop it now. This is my time. It ends here. God's glory begins today!"

The catastrophe of noise in Waters' head had turned into a rhythm, a pattern, more curious than painful. It was soothing now, almost musical. His vision cleared, and he saw Cruz differently: hideous, evil, and almost serpentine.

The lights dimmed briefly and phones began to vibrate everywhere. Mackey's virus had finished its work. For the first time in decades, anyone could call anyone else. And they did, massively, spontaneously. They called loved ones and friends, business associates and schoolmates, then strangers. They just dialed randomly and talked to whoever answered, no matter the language difference. Mackey's program linked voice recognition databases with language translators. All conversation arrived in the listener's native language no matter how it was spoken.

Stacey and her husband huddled together in the hallway of H2, calling people to tell them they were okay. They soon discovered they didn't need phone numbers. The network had voice recognition, and it knew everything about everyone. You could ask for your "brother Bob" and it knew who that was.

"Yeah, pretty screwed up," said Stacey to her business partner, who was at his private island. "The funny thing is that both sides think God is on their side. I mean, not funny *that* way, but you know. Even worse, what if God actually *was* on your side? You'd be on the dumb team."

"How can you say God is dumb?" asked Stacey's business partner. "Maybe you just don't understand what he wants."

"Let me put it this way. Let's say God designed you. He's all-powerful, right, so he can design you to be *any way* he wants."

"Right."

"So, here's my question: If God is so smart, why do you fart?"

The business partner was silent for a moment, absorbing the concept. Then he laughed. "I have to call someone and use that line. Do you mind if I say I thought of it?"

"It's all yours, goober."

"Don't call me goober."

"Whatever. Who are you going to call?"

"I have a minister friend. We're always arguing about this stuff. I'm trying to figure out what's wrong with your point, but I don't see it."

"Don't hurt yourself trying. By the way, I'm glad you didn't die yet."

"Same right back at you."

FINDING A DONOR

The bullet tore through General Cruz's skull and lodged itself in the hospital wall. Waters watched the general's body crumple at the feet of the dark-haired doctor.

"I found a donor," Waters said, holstering his weapon.

The doctor stared in horror. "How will you explain—?"

"That's *my* problem," said Waters. "*Your* problem is on that table."

"The old man is brain-dead. There's no hope."

"I'm not so sure," said Waters, helping the doctor lift Cruz's body to an operating table. "He doesn't think like us."

THIRTY YEARS LATER

Years later, historians disagreed about why the war suddenly ended. There was no surrender, no victory, just a universal and abrupt shift in motivation. Both sides lost their reason to fight. Most scholars pointed to Cruz's death as a turning point, speculating that the loss of leadership changed everything. Others pointed out that the fighting had mostly stopped before anyone knew Cruz was dead.

The young deliveryman listened intently as the Avatar explained what happened during the dark days of the Religion War. The Avatar rocked gently in his wooden chair, speaking softly, his borrowed heart nearing its limits. The fireplace light played on his ancient features while a tattered red plaid blanket warmed his legs. At times the young man didn't believe what he was hearing. Other times he had goose bumps and felt electricity throughout his body. He had delivered his package and it was time to leave, but he couldn't. He belonged in this room, this house. It was his time to listen and learn.

The Avatar explained that after all terror attacks ended, the GIC database found a new purpose. People loved the fact that Mackey's program allowed anyone on Earth to call anyone else.

Ideas and knowledge flowed continuously and freely. Anything known by one person was available to all. People observed the results of their actions, and they fed that knowledge back to the whole, thus changing the collective consciousness. It was later discovered that Mackey's program would destroy all calling history records as soon as they were created, ensuring total privacy.

"Is that why our phone calls don't cost us anything?" asked the young man.

The Avatar confirmed that the best minds in the telecommunications industry had tried to stop Mackey's program, to limit its obsession with privacy at least enough so they would know whom to bill. It was too late. Mackey's program had no physical form, changing by the minute, like a benevolent spirit in the hardware. No one ever learned how Mackey had created such a program. It seemed to be based not on rules, like all code before it, but on morality. It had a sense of right and wrong, and it seemed to learn. It developed preferences, and it devoured any code that opposed it. It was Mackey's preferences, disembodied, permanent.

Eventually, governments funded all communications costs because there was no way to identify how much of the network any particular customer was using. In time, people wondered how the world had ever tolerated limits on communication. The days of restricted communication were viewed as the darkest period in human history, when people had more technical ability than awareness.

The major religions changed after the war. "Modernized" was the word most often used for the disintegration of primitive beliefs. The free flow of ideas caused dangerous religious thoughts

174

to perish under the weight of common sense. Most notably, the idea that God was limited by a human personality, with human wants, and human intelligence, evaporated. Now the mental health profession handled people who believed that God was talking to them directly; the voting public never got a chance to elect such people, whether they were charismatic or not. Religions came to be seen as traditions that lent flavor to holidays and encouraged good behavior, nothing more.

The public didn't know who said it first, but it was the most powerful question in human history. In nine words it overturned centuries of tortured logic and magical thinking. It pushed superstition into a cage and gave common sense room to maneuver. The cause of the Religion War sprung from one colossal religious misunderstanding: that God *thinks like humans,* except smarter, and that we humans can comprehend his intent. That crippling misunderstanding was swept away in a single wave of clarity. The question was translated into thousands of languages, published billions of times. In English it was "If God is so smart, why do you fart?"

Every living person knew the question and remembered where they first heard it. It put everything in perspective, cutting across age, education, and background. Until that day, the world was held hostage by an imagined supernatural being who had the curious qualities of being all-powerful, yet being unable or unwilling to make an odor-free human. That absurdity and a thousand similar ones had been accepted as harmless truths until the Religion War made it clear that unbridled superstition would destroy civilization. The system of human ideas had frozen. It needed to be cleared and restarted. When Mackey's GoD program removed the government filters from the worldwide phone network, the nine-word question swept across civilization in a matter of hours. Everyone who heard it felt the need to repeat it to someone close, someone who would listen. The question spread from person to person along unbroken chains of influence, until every role model and mentor had spoken with every person in his or her sphere.

It wasn't the wisdom of the question that made it so powerful; philosophers had posed better questions for aeons. It was the packaging—the marketing, if you will—the repeatability and simplicity, the timing, the zeitgeist, and in the end, the fact that everyone eventually heard it from someone whose opinion they trusted. The question was short, provocative, and cast in the language of international commerce that almost everyone understood—English. Most important, and generally overlooked by historians: It rhymed and it was funny. Once you heard it, you could never forget it. It looped in the brain, gaining the weight and feel of truth with each repetition. Human brains have a limited capacity for logic and evidence. Throughout time, repetition and frequency were how people decided what was most true. The question "If God is so smart, why do you fart?" played over and over in the minds of billions of people, especially the children who repeated it ad nauseam on the playgrounds and in schools. It appeared on bumper stickers, shirts, greeting cards, and products of all kinds.

Yet, despite the new disdain of superstition, almost no one argued the existence of God, only the details. Some said God was Mackey's program. Others said it was the network, or the way the network connected the intelligence of all humanity, forming a superconsciousness. The Avatar knew, and soon the young deliveryman would know: God is everything, all the matter and empty space that now exists, or ever will exist. He expresses his preference in the invisible workings of gravity, probability, and ideas. God is that which is unstoppable, permanent, all-powerful, and by its own standards perfect. God was in no hurry. He was re-forming. He didn't think in the way that humans do, as that is unnecessary for an entity whose preferences are identical to reality. Humans think in order to survive and entertain themselves. God has no need for a tool that is useful only to the frail and unsatisfied.

Stacey never knew that she was the Prime Influencer, the reboot button for the universe. When the Avatar recovered from his heart transplant and pieced together what had happened, he thought it would be better if she never knew her role. For years, Stacey insisted to friends that she had invented the saying "If God is so smart, why do you fart?" No one believed her. In time she came to think that she must have first heard it someplace and forgotten. She also never knew that as the Prime Influencer she caused pink to become the most common hair color for women, or that she was the reason virtually every home now had a pet chicken. And she certainly had no idea that she selected the last seven American presidents. She thought perhaps she had a knack for guessing who would win, never suspecting that she caused the outcome.

The Avatar finally understood why the patterns he had felt outside the GIC building were confused. There had been two patterns intersecting on that street. He needed both Mackey and Stacey to change the world. It seemed obvious now.

The young man still had much to learn. He had many questions, and that was okay, because he would be there all night, and longer. The Avatar would talk until nothing was left to say, no question unanswered, no mystery unsolved. The young man didn't yet realize that he was quitting his job as a package deliveryman. Money wouldn't be a problem, as he would soon inherit the biggest personal fortune in the world. But he would live alone, preparing himself for the day when evil would rise again.

QUESTIONS TO PONDER

1. If you suspected you were deluded, how could you find out for sure?

2. Are humans the product of a skilled or an unskilled designer?

3. Would an omnipotent being need to *think* in the way that people understand it? Or is thinking unnecessary for a timeless, indestructible being whose preferences are the same as reality?

4. Why would God be so unclear about what book or books he authored?

5. Is consciousness anything more than a continual process of imagining, acting, observing the impact of the action, and imagining again with new information?

6. The dictionary defines "faith" as belief without evidence. It defines "stupidity" as unreasoned thinking. Is belief without evidence a form of unreasoned thinking?

7. Can the impact of your actions rippling into the future be considered an immortal soul?

8. Could atheists and believers accept the same definition of God?